W0008851

DOVER·THRIFT·EDITIONS

The Queen of Spades and Other Stories

ALEXANDER PUSHKIN

Translated from the Russian by T. Keane

DOVER PUBLICATIONS, INC.
New York

DOVER THRIFT EDITIONS

GENERAL EDITOR: STANLEY APPELBAUM
EDITOR OF THIS VOLUME: THOMAS CROFTS

Copyright

Copyright © 1994 by Dover Publications, Inc.
All rights reserved under Pan American and International Copyright Conventions.

Bibliographical Note

This Dover edition, first published in 1994, is an unabridged republication of stories originally appearing in the 1916 edition of *The Prose Tales of Alexander Poushkin*, translated from the Russian by T. Keane, G. Bell and Sons, Ltd, London (original edition, 1894). Some explanatory footnotes and an introductory Note have been specially prepared for the present edition.

Library of Congress Cataloging-in-Publication Data

Pushkin, Aleksandr Sergeevich, 1799–1837.
    [Short stories. English. Selections]
    The queen of spades, and other stories / Alexander Pushkin; translated from the Russian by T. Keane.
    p.   cm. — (Dover thrift editions)
    "Unabridged republication of stories originally appearing in the 1916 edition of The prose tales of Alexander Poushkin"—T.p. verso.
    ISBN 0-486-28054-3 (pbk.)
    1. Pushkin, Aleksandr Sergeevich, 1799–1837—Translations into English. I. Keane, T. II. Title. III. Series.
PG3347.A2   1994
891.73'3—dc20
                                                94-16532
                                                  CIP

Manufactured in the United States of America
Dover Publications, Inc., 31 East 2nd Street, Mineola, N.Y. 11501

Note

ALEXANDER SERGEYEVICH PUSHKIN (1799–1837) could without exaggeration be called the founding father of modern Russian literature. He was the nation's first poet to achieve international fame writing in his mother tongue (educated Russians then used mainly French and German); his play *Boris Godunov* was transformed by the composer Modest Mussorgsky (1835–1881) into Russia's most admired opera; and he created a role that itself became a Russian national treasure, that of the subversive writer.

Pushkin was more than once jailed for his poetry, its content judged by Imperial censors to be either treasonous ("The Upas Tree," a searing indictment of the Tsarist regime) or morally corrupt ("The Gavriliad," a raffish burlesque of the Annunciation). Finally, Tsar Nicholas I, while encouraging the poet to write, burdened him with his own Imperial censor, a Count Benckendorff, whom Pushkin openly insulted and often hoodwinked by inscribing "Translated from the Latin" at the head of certain manuscripts.

While Pushkin's greatest contributions may be in the medium of verse, his small body of prose fiction, which includes novels, short stories and folktales, rewards investigation. The stories included here represent two distinct aspects of Pushkin's fiction writing. "The Queen of Spades" (1833–1834) reflects, in style as well as in substance, the cosmopolitan Russia of the nineteenth century: urbane, card-playing officers, fancy dress balls and countesses. The other stories included here, written a short time earlier, are known collectively as *The Tales of the Late P. Belkin* after the fictional author under whose name Pushkin published them (his first printed stories). Set for the most part far from Moscow and St. Petersburg, these portray the character of rural Russia: provincial government functionaries, poor soldiers and artisans, plump land-owners and their beguiling young daughters.

For this edition, the editors have provided a handful of new footnotes — translations of French phrases, card-game terminology and the like. These new notes appear within square brackets and are starred and daggered, whereas the notes provided by the translator Keane appear with their original numbering.

Contents

The Queen of Spades   1

The Tales of the Late P. Belkin

An Amateur Peasant Girl   25

The Shot   43

The Snowstorm   55

The Postmaster   67

The Coffin-Maker   79

The Queen of Spades.

CHAPTER I.

THERE WAS A card party at the rooms of Naroumoff of the Horse Guards. The long winter night passed away imperceptibly, and it was five o'clock in the morning before the company sat down to supper. Those who had won, ate with a good appetite; the others sat staring absently at their empty plates. When the champagne appeared, however, the conversation became more animated, and all took a part in it.

"And how did you fare, Sourin?" asked the host.

"Oh, I lost, as usual. I must confess that I am unlucky: I play mirandole,* I always keep cool, I never allow anything to put me out, and yet I always lose!"

"And you did not once allow yourself to be tempted to back the red? . . . Your firmness astonishes me."

"But what do you think of Hermann?" said one of the guests, pointing to a young Engineer: "he has never had a card in his hand in his life, he has never in his life laid a wager, and yet he sits here till five o'clock in the morning watching our play."

"Play interests me very much," said Hermann: "but I am not in the position to sacrifice the necessary in the hope of winning the superfluous."

"Hermann is a German: he is economical—that is all!" observed Tomsky. "But if there is one person that I cannot understand, it is my grandmother, the Countess Anna Fedorovna."

"How so?" inquired the guests.

"I cannot understand," continued Tomsky, "how it is that my grandmother does not punt."†

"What is there remarkable about an old lady of eighty not punting?" said Naroumoff.

"Then you do not know the reason why?"

"No, really; haven't the faintest idea."

"Oh! then listen. You must know that, about sixty years ago, my grandmother went to Paris, where she created quite a sensation. People used to run after her to catch a glimpse of the 'Muscovite Venus.'

* [Not increasing the stakes.]
† [To play against the banker, in faro.]

Richelieu made love to her, and my grandmother maintains that he almost blew out his brains in consequence of her cruelty. At that time ladies used to play at faro. On one occasion at the Court, she lost a very considerable sum to the Duke of Orleans. On returning home, my grandmother removed the patches from her face, took off her hoops, informed my grandfather of her loss at the gaming-table, and ordered him to pay the money. My deceased grandfather, as far as I remember, was a sort of house-steward to my grandmother. He dreaded her like fire; but, on hearing of such a heavy loss, he almost went out of his mind; he calculated the various sums she had lost, and pointed out to her that in six months she had spent half a million of francs, that neither their Moscow nor Saratoff estates were in Paris, and finally refused point blank to pay the debt. My grandmother gave him a box on the ear and slept by herself as a sign of her displeasure. The next day she sent for her husband, hoping that this domestic punishment had produced an effect upon him, but she found him inflexible. For the first time in her life, she entered into reasonings and explanations with him, thinking to be able to convince him by pointing out to him that there are debts and debts, and that there is a great difference between a Prince and a coachmaker. But it was all in vain, my grandfather still remained obdurate. But the matter did not rest there. My grandmother did not know what to do. She had shortly before become acquainted with a very remarkable man. You have heard of Count St. Germain,* about whom so many marvellous stories are told. You know that he represented himself as the Wandering Jew, as the discoverer of the elixir of life, of the philosopher's stone, and so forth. Some laughed at him as a charlatan; but Casanova, in his memoirs, says that he was a spy. But be that as it may, St. Germain, in spite of the mystery surrounding him, was a very fascinating person, and was much sought after in the best circles of society. Even to this day my grandmother retains an affectionate recollection of him, and becomes quite angry if anyone speaks disrespectfully of him. My grandmother knew that St. Germain had large sums of money at his disposal. She resolved to have recourse to him, and she wrote a letter to him asking him to come to her without delay. The queer old man immediately waited upon her and found her overwhelmed with grief. She described to him in the blackest colours the barbarity of her husband, and ended by declaring that her whole hope depended upon his friendship and amiability.

"St. Germain reflected.

---

* [Famous adventurer, died 1784.]

" 'I could advance you the sum you want,' said he; 'but I know that you would not rest easy until you had paid me back, and I should not like to bring fresh troubles upon you. But there is another way of getting out of your difficulty: you can win back your money.'

" 'But, my dear Count,' replied my grandmother, 'I tell you that I haven't any money left.'

" 'Money is not necessary,' replied St. Germain: 'be pleased to listen to me.'

"Then he revealed to her a secret, for which each of us would give a good deal . . .''

The young officers listened with increased attention. Tomsky lit his pipe, puffed away for a moment and then continued:

"That same evening my grandmother went to Versailles to the *jeu de la reine.* * The Duke of Orleans kept the bank; my grandmother excused herself in an off-handed manner for not having yet paid her debt, by inventing some little story, and then began to play against him. She chose three cards and played them one after the other: all three won *sonika,*† and my grandmother recovered every farthing that she had lost."

"Mere chance!" said one of the guests.

"A tale!" observed Hermann.

"Perhaps they were marked cards!" said a third.

"I do not think so," replied Tomsky gravely.

"What!" said Naroumoff, "you have a grandmother who knows how to hit upon three lucky cards in succession, and you have never yet succeeded in getting the secret of it out of her?"

"That's the deuce of it!" replied Tomsky: "she had four sons, one of whom was my father; all four were determined gamblers, and yet not to one of them did she ever reveal her secret, although it would not have been a bad thing either for them or for me. But this is what I heard from my uncle, Count Ivan Ilitch, and he assured me, on his honour, that it was true. The late Chaplitsky — the same who died in poverty after having squandered millions — once lost, in his youth, about three hundred thousand roubles — to Zoritch,‡ if I remember rightly. He was in despair. My grandmother, who was always very severe upon the extravagance of young men, took pity, however, upon Chaplitsky. She gave him three cards, telling him to play them one after the other, at the same

* [The Queen's card party.]
† [Breaking the bank.]
‡ [A favorite of Catherine the Great.]

time exacting from him a solemn promise that he would never play at cards again as long as he lived. Chaplitsky then went to his victorious opponent, and they began a fresh game. On the first card he staked fifty thousand roubles and won *sonika*; he doubled the stake and won again, till at last, by pursuing the same tactics, he won back more than he had lost . . .

"But it is time to go to bed: it is a quarter to six already."

And indeed it was already beginning to dawn: the young men emptied their glasses and then took leave of each other.

Chapter II.

The old Countess A—— was seated in her dressing-room in front of her looking-glass. Three waiting-maids stood around her. One held a small pot of rouge, another a box of hair-pins, and the third a tall cap with bright red ribbons. The Countess had no longer the slightest pretensions to beauty, but she still preserved the habits of her youth, dressed in strict accordance with the fashion of seventy years before, and made as long and as careful a toilette as she would have done sixty years previously. Near the window, at an embroidery frame, sat a young lady, her ward.

"Good morning, grandmamma," said a young officer, entering the room. "*Bonjour, Mademoiselle Lise*. Grandmamma, I want to ask you something."

"What is it, Paul?"

"I want you to let me introduce one of my friends to you, and to allow me to bring him to the ball on Friday."

"Bring him direct to the ball and introduce him to me there. Were you at B——'s yesterday?"

"Yes; everything went off very pleasantly, and dancing was kept up until five o'clock. How charming Eletskaia was!"

"But, my dear, what is there charming about her? Isn't she like her grandmother, the Princess Daria Petrovna? By the way, she must be very old, the Princess Daria Petrovna."

"How do you mean, old?" cried Tomsky thoughtlessly; "she died seven years ago."

The young lady raised her head and made a sign to the young officer. He then remembered that the old Countess was never to be informed of the death of any of her contemporaries, and he bit his lips. But the old Countess heard the news with the greatest indifference.

"Dead!" said she; "and I did not know it. We were appointed maids of honour at the same time, and when we were presented to the Empress . . ."

And the Countess for the hundredth time related to her grandson one of her anecdotes.

"Come, Paul," said she, when she had finished her story, "help me to get up. Lizanka,[1] where is my snuff-box?"

And the Countess with her three maids went behind a screen to finish her toilette. Tomsky was left alone with the young lady.

"Who is the gentleman you wish to introduce to the Countess?" asked Lizaveta Ivanovna in a whisper.

"Naroumoff. Do you know him?"

"No. Is he a soldier or a civilian?"

"A soldier."

"Is he in the Engineers?"

"No, in the Cavalry. What made you think that he was in the Engineers?"

The young lady smiled, but made no reply.

"Paul," cried the Countess from behind the screen, "send me some new novel, only pray don't let it be one of the present day style."

"What do you mean, grandmother?"

"That is, a novel, in which the hero strangles neither his father nor his mother, and in which there are no drowned bodies. I have a great horror of drowned persons."

"There are no such novels nowadays. Would you like a Russian one?"

"Are there any Russian novels? Send me one, my dear, pray send me one!"

"Good-bye, grandmother: I am in a hurry. . . . Good-bye, Lizaveta Ivanovna. What made you think that Naroumoff was in the Engineers?"

And Tomsky left the boudoir.

Lizaveta Ivanovna was left alone: she laid aside her work and began to look out of the window. A few moments afterwards, at a corner house on the other side of the street, a young officer appeared. A deep blush covered her cheeks; she took up her work again and bent her head down over the frame. At the same moment the Countess returned completely dressed.

"Order the carriage, Lizaveta," said she; "we will go out for a drive."

Lizaveta arose from the frame and began to arrange her work.

[1] Diminutive of Lizaveta (Elizabeth).

"What is the matter with you, my child, are you deaf?" cried the Countess. "Order the carriage to be got ready at once."

"I will do so this moment," replied the young lady, hastening into the ante-room.

A servant entered and gave the Countess some books from Prince Paul Alexandrovitch.

"Tell him that I am much obliged to him," said the Countess. "Lizaveta! Lizaveta! where are you running to?"

"I am going to dress."

"There is plenty of time, my dear. Sit down here. Open the first volume and read to me aloud."

Her companion took the book and read a few lines.

"Louder," said the Countess. "What is the matter with you, my child? Have you lost your voice? Wait—give me that footstool—a little nearer—that will do!"

Lizaveta read two more pages. The Countess yawned.

"Put the book down," said she: "what a lot of nonsense! Send it back to Prince Paul with my thanks. . . . But where is the carriage?"

"The carriage is ready," said Lizaveta, looking out into the street.

"How is it that you are not dressed?" said the Countess: "I must always wait for you. It is intolerable, my dear!"

Liza hastened to her room. She had not been there two minutes, before the Countess began to ring with all her might. The three waiting-maids came running in at one door and the valet at another.

"How is it that you cannot hear me when I ring for you?" said the Countess. "Tell Lizaveta Ivanovna that I am waiting for her."

Lizaveta returned with her hat and cloak on.

"At last you are here!" said the Countess. "But why such an elaborate toilette? Whom do you intend to captivate? What sort of weather is it? It seems rather windy."

"No, Your Ladyship, it is very calm," replied the valet.

"You never think of what you are talking about. Open the window. So it is: windy and bitterly cold. Unharness the horses. Lizaveta, we won't go out—there was no need for you to deck yourself like that."

"What a life is mine!" thought Lizaveta Ivanovna.

And, in truth, Lizaveta Ivanovna was a very unfortunate creature. "The bread of the stranger is bitter," says Dante, "and his staircase hard to climb." But who can know what the bitterness of dependence is so well as the poor companion of an old lady of quality? The Countess A—— had by no means a bad heart, but she was capricious, like a woman who had been spoilt by the world, as well as being avaricious and egotistical, like all old people who have seen their best days, and whose thoughts are with the past and not the present. She participated in all the vanities of the great world, went to balls, where she sat in a corner, painted and dressed in old-fashioned style, like a deformed but indispensable ornament of the ball-room; all the guests on entering approached her and made a profound bow, as if in accordance with a set ceremony, but after that nobody took any further notice of her. She received the whole town at her house, and observed the strictest etiquette, although she could no longer recognize the faces of people. Her numerous domestics, growing fat and old in her ante-chamber and servants' hall, did just as they liked, and vied with each other in robbing the aged Countess in the most bare-faced manner. Lizaveta Ivanovna was the martyr of the household. She made tea, and was reproached with using too much sugar; she read novels aloud to the Countess, and the faults of the author were visited upon her head; she accompanied the Countess in her walks, and was held answerable for the weather or the state of the pavement. A salary was attached to the post, but she very rarely received it, although she was expected to dress like everybody else, that is to say, like very few indeed. In society she played the most pitiable rôle. Everybody knew her, and nobody paid her any attention. At balls she danced only when a partner was wanted, and ladies would only take hold of her arm when it was necessary to lead her out of the room to attend to their dresses. She was very self-conscious, and felt her position keenly, and she looked about her with impatience for a deliverer to come to her rescue; but the young men, calculating in their giddiness, honoured her with but very little attention, although Lizaveta Ivanovna was a hundred times prettier than the bare-faced and cold-hearted marriageable girls around whom they hovered. Many a time did she quietly slink away from the glittering but wearisome drawing-room, to go and cry in her own poor little room, in which stood a screen, a chest of drawers, a looking-glass and a painted bedstead, and where a tallow candle burnt feebly in a copper candlestick.

One morning—this was about two days after the evening party described at the beginning of this story, and a week previous to the scene at which we have just assisted—Lizaveta Ivanovna was seated near the window at her embroidery frame, when, happening to look out into the street, she caught sight of a young Engineer officer, standing motionless with his eyes fixed upon her window. She lowered her head and went on again with her work. About five minutes afterwards she looked out again—the young officer was still standing in the same place. Not being in the habit of coquetting with passing officers, she did not continue to gaze out into the street, but went on sewing for a couple of hours, without raising her head. Dinner was announced. She rose up and began to put her embroidery away, but glancing casually out of the window, she perceived the officer again. This seemed to her very strange. After dinner she went to the window with a certain feeling of uneasiness, but the officer was no longer there — and she thought no more about him.

A couple of days afterwards, just as she was stepping into the carriage with the Countess, she saw him again. He was standing close behind the door, with his face half-concealed by his fur collar, but his dark eyes sparkled beneath his cap. Lizaveta felt alarmed, though she knew not why, and she trembled as she seated herself in the carriage.

On returning home, she hastened to the window — the officer was standing in his accustomed place, with his eyes fixed upon her. She drew back, a prey to curiosity and agitated by a feeling which was quite new to her.

From that time forward not a day passed without the young officer making his appearance under the window at the customary hour, and between him and her there was established a sort of mute acquaintance. Sitting in her place at work, she used to feel his approach; and raising her head, she would look at him longer and longer each day. The young man seemed to be very grateful to her: she saw with the sharp eye of youth, how a sudden flush covered his pale cheeks each time that their glances met. After about a week she commenced to smile at him. . . .

When Tomsky asked permission of his grandmother the Countess to present one of his friends to her, the young girl's heart beat violently. But hearing that Naroumoff was not an Engineer, she regretted that by her thoughtless question, she had betrayed her secret to the volatile Tomsky.

Hermann was the son of a German who had become a naturalized Russian, and from whom he had inherited a small capital. Being firmly convinced of the necessity of preserving his independence, Hermann did not touch his private income, but lived on his pay, without allowing himself the slightest luxury. Moreover, he was reserved and ambitious, and his companions rarely had an opportunity of making merry at the expense of his extreme parsimony. He had strong passions and an ardent imagination, but his firmness of disposition preserved him from the ordinary errors of young men. Thus, though a gamester at heart, he never touched a card, for he considered his position did not allow him — as he said — "to risk the necessary in the hope of winning the superfluous," yet he would sit for nights together at the card table and follow with feverish anxiety the different turns of the game.

The story of the three cards had produced a powerful impression upon his imagination, and all night long he could think of nothing else. "If," he thought to himself the following evening, as he walked along the streets of St. Petersburg, "if the old Countess would but reveal her secret to me! if she would only tell me the names of the three winning cards. Why should I not try my fortune? I must get introduced to her and win her favour — become her lover. . . . But all that will take time, and she is eighty-seven years old: she might be dead in a week, in a couple of days even! . . . But the story itself: can it really be true? . . . No! Economy, temperance and industry: those are my three winning cards; by means of them I shall be able to double my capital — increase it sevenfold, and procure for myself ease and independence."

Musing in this manner, he walked on until he found himself in one of the principal streets of St. Petersburg, in front of a house of antiquated architecture. The street was blocked with equipages; carriages one after the other drew up in front of the brilliantly illuminated doorway. At one moment there stepped out on to the pavement the well-shaped little foot of some young beauty, at another the heavy boot of a cavalry officer, and then the silk stockings and shoes of a member of the diplomatic world. Furs and cloaks passed in rapid succession before the gigantic porter at the entrance.

Hermann stopped. "Whose house is this?" he asked of the watchman at the corner.

"The Countess A——'s," replied the watchman.

Hermann started. The strange story of the three cards again presented itself to his imagination. He began walking up and down before the house, thinking of its owner and her strange secret. Returning late to his modest lodging, he could not go to sleep for a long time, and when at last he did doze off, he could dream of nothing but cards, green tables, piles of banknotes and heaps of ducats. He played one card after the other, winning uninterruptedly, and then he gathered up the gold and filled his pockets with the notes. When he woke up late the next morning, he sighed over the loss of his imaginary wealth, and then sallying out into the town, he found himself once more in front of the Countess's residence. Some unknown power seemed to have attracted him thither. He stopped and looked up at the windows. At one of these he saw a head with luxuriant black hair, which was bent down probably over some book or an embroidery frame. The head was raised. Hermann saw a fresh complexion and a pair of dark eyes. That moment decided his fate.

CHAPTER III.

LIZAVETA IVANOVNA had scarcely taken off her hat and cloak, when the Countess sent for her and again ordered her to get the carriage ready. The vehicle drew up before the door, and they prepared to take their seats. Just at the moment when two footmen were assisting the old lady to enter the carriage, Lizaveta saw her Engineer standing close beside the wheel; he grasped her hand; alarm caused her to lose her presence of mind, and the young man disappeared — but not before he had left a letter between her fingers. She concealed it in her glove, and during the whole of the drive she neither saw nor heard anything. It was the custom of the Countess, when out for an airing in her carriage, to be constantly asking such questions as: "Who was that person that met us just now? What is the name of this bridge? What is written on that signboard?" On this occasion, however, Lizaveta returned such vague and absurd answers, that the Countess became angry with her.

"What is the matter with you, my dear?" she exclaimed. "Have you taken leave of your senses, or what is it? Do you not hear me or understand what I say? . . . Heaven be thanked, I am still in my right mind and speak plainly enough!"

Lizaveta Ivanovna did not hear her. On returning home she ran to her room, and drew the letter out of her glove: it was not sealed. Lizaveta read it. The letter contained a declaration of love; it was tender, respectful, and copied word for word from a German novel. But Lizaveta did not know anything of the German language, and she was quite delighted.

For all that, the letter caused her to feel exceedingly uneasy. For the first time in her life she was entering into secret and confidential relations with a young man. His boldness alarmed her. She reproached herself for her imprudent behaviour, and knew not what to do. Should she cease to sit at the window and, by assuming an appearance of indifference towards him, put a check upon the young officer's desire for further acquaintance with her? Should she send his letter back to him, or should she answer him in a cold and decided manner? There was nobody to whom she could turn in her perplexity, for she had neither female friend nor adviser. . . . At length she resolved to reply to him.

She sat down at her little writing-table, took pen and paper, and began to think. Several times she began her letter, and then tore it up: the way she had expressed herself seemed to her either too inviting or too cold and decisive. At last she succeeded in writing a few lines with which she felt satisfied.

"I am convinced," she wrote, "that your intentions are honourable, and that you do not wish to offend me by any imprudent behaviour, but our acquaintance must not begin in such a manner. I return you your letter, and I hope that I shall never have any cause to complain of this undeserved slight."

The next day, as soon as Hermann made his appearance, Lizaveta rose from her embroidery, went into the drawing-room, opened the ventilator and threw the letter into the street, trusting that the young officer would have the perception to pick it up.

Hermann hastened forward, picked it up and then repaired to a confectioner's shop. Breaking the seal of the envelope, he found inside it his own letter and Lizaveta's reply. He had expected this, and he returned home, his mind deeply occupied with his intrigue.

Three days afterwards, a bright-eyed young girl from a milliner's establishment brought Lizaveta a letter. Lizaveta opened it with great uneasiness, fearing that it was a demand for money, when suddenly she recognized Hermann's handwriting.

"You have made a mistake, my dear," said she: "this letter is not for me."

"Oh, yes, it is for you," replied the girl, smiling very knowingly. "Have the goodness to read it."

Lizaveta glanced at the letter. Hermann requested an interview.

"It cannot be," she cried, alarmed at the audacious request, and the manner in which it was made. "This letter is certainly not for me."

And she tore it into fragments.

"If the letter was not for you, why have you torn it up?" said the girl. "I should have given it back to the person who sent it."

"Be good enough, my dear," said Lizaveta, disconcerted by this remark, "not to bring me any more letters for the future, and tell the person who sent you that he ought to be ashamed. . . ."

But Hermann was not the man to be thus put off. Every day Lizaveta received from him a letter, sent now in this way, now in that. They were no longer translated from the German. Hermann wrote them under the inspiration of passion, and spoke in his own language, and they bore full testimony to the inflexibility of his desire and the disordered condition of his uncontrollable imagination. Lizaveta no longer thought of sending them back to him: she became intoxicated with them and began to reply to them, and little by little her answers became longer and more affectionate. At last she threw out of the window to him the following letter:

"This evening there is going to be a ball at the Embassy. The Countess will be there. We shall remain until two o'clock. You have now an opportunity of seeing me alone. As soon as the Countess is gone, the servants will very probably go out, and there will be nobody left but the Swiss, but he usually goes to sleep in his lodge. Come about half-past eleven. Walk straight upstairs. If you meet anybody in the ante-room, ask if the Countess is at home. You will be told 'No,' in which case there will be nothing left for you to do but to go away again. But it is most probable that you will meet nobody. The maidservants will all be together in one room. On leaving the ante-room, turn to the left, and walk straight on until you reach the Countess's bedroom. In the bedroom, behind a screen, you will find two doors: the one on the right leads to a cabinet, which the Countess never enters; the one on the left leads to a corridor, at the end of which is a little winding staircase; this leads to my room."

Hermann trembled like a tiger, as he waited for the appointed time to arrive. At ten o'clock in the evening he was already in front of the Countess's house. The weather was terrible; the wind blew with great violence; the sleety snow fell in large flakes; the lamps emitted a feeble light, the streets were deserted; from time to time a sledge, drawn by a sorry-looking hack, passed by, on the look-out for a belated passenger. Hermann was enveloped in a thick overcoat, and felt neither wind nor snow.

At last the Countess's carriage drew up. Hermann saw two footmen carry out in their arms the bent form of the old lady, wrapped in sable fur, and immediately behind her, clad in a warm mantle, and with her head ornamented with a wreath of fresh flowers, followed Lizaveta. The door was closed. The carriage rolled away heavily through the yielding snow. The porter shut the street-door; the windows became dark.

Hermann began walking up and down near the deserted house; at length he stopped under a lamp, and glanced at his watch: it was twenty minutes past eleven. He remained standing under a lamp, his eyes fixed upon the watch, impatiently waiting for the remaining minutes to pass. At half-past eleven precisely, Hermann ascended the steps of the house, and made his way into the brightly-illuminated vestibule. The porter was not there. Hermann hastily ascended the staircase, opened the door of the ante-room and saw a footman sitting asleep in an antique chair by the side of a lamp. With a light firm step Hermann passed by him. The drawing-room and dining-room were in darkness, but a feeble reflection penetrated thither from the lamp in the ante-room.

* * *

Hermann reached the Countess's bedroom. Before a shrine, which was full of old images, a golden lamp was burning. Faded stuffed chairs and divans with soft cushions stood in melancholy symmetry around the room, the walls of which were hung with China silk. On one side of the room hung two portraits painted in Paris by Madame Lebrun.* One of these represented a stout, red-faced man of about forty years of age in a bright-green uniform and with a star upon his breast; the other — a beautiful young woman, with an aquiline nose, forehead curls and a rose in her powdered hair. In the corners stood porcelain shepherds and shepherdesses, dining-room clocks from the workshop of the celebrated Leroy, bandboxes, roulettes, fans and the various playthings for the amusement of ladies that were in vogue at the end of the last century, when Montgolfier's balloons and Mesmer's magnetism were the rage. Hermann stepped behind the screen. At the back of it stood a little iron bedstead; on the right was the door which led to the cabinet; on the left — the other which led to the corridor. He opened the latter, and saw the little winding staircase which led to the room of the poor companion. . . . But he retraced his steps and entered the dark cabinet.

The time passed slowly. All was still. The clock in the drawing-room struck twelve; the strokes echoed through the room one after the other, and everything was quiet again. Hermann stood leaning against the cold stove. He was calm; his heart beat regularly, like that of a man resolved upon a dangerous but inevitable undertaking. One o'clock in the morning struck; then two; and he heard the distant noise of carriage-wheels. An involuntary agitation took possession of him. The carriage drew near and stopped. He heard the sound of the carriage-steps being let down. All was bustle within the house. The servants were running hither and thither, there was a confusion of voices, and the rooms were lit up. Three antiquated chamber-maids entered the bedroom, and they were shortly afterwards followed by the Countess who, more dead than alive, sank into a Voltaire armchair.† Hermann peeped through a chink. Lizaveta Ivanovna passed close by him, and he heard her hurried steps as she hastened up the little spiral staircase. For a moment his heart was assailed by something like a pricking of conscience, but the emotion was only transitory, and his heart became petrified as before.

The Countess began to undress before her looking-glass. Her rose-bedecked cap was taken off, and then her powdered wig was removed

* [Elisabeth Vigée-Lebrun, 1755–1842.]
† [Soft armchair with high back and low seat.]

from off her white and closely-cut hair. Hairpins fell in showers around her. Her yellow satin dress, brocaded with silver, fell down at her swollen feet.

Hermann was a witness of the repugnant mysteries of her toilette; at last the Countess was in her night-cap and dressing-gown, and in this costume, more suitable to her age, she appeared less hideous and deformed.

Like all old people in general, the Countess suffered from sleeplessness. Having undressed, she seated herself at the window in a Voltaire armchair and dismissed her maids. The candles were taken away, and once more the room was left with only one lamp burning in it. The Countess sat there looking quite yellow, mumbling with her flaccid lips and swaying to and fro. Her dull eyes expressed complete vacancy of mind, and, looking at her, one would have thought that the rocking of her body was not a voluntary action of her own, but was produced by the action of some concealed galvanic mechanism.

Suddenly the death-like face assumed an inexplicable expression. The lips ceased to tremble, the eyes became animated: before the Countess stood an unknown man.

"Do not be alarmed, for Heaven's sake, do not be alarmed!" said he in a low but distinct voice. "I have no intention of doing you any harm, I have only come to ask a favour of you."

The old woman looked at him in silence, as if she had not heard what he had said. Hermann thought that she was deaf, and, bending down towards her ear, he repeated what he had said. The aged Countess remained silent as before.

"You can insure the happiness of my life," continued Hermann, "and it will cost you nothing. I know that you can name three cards in order——"

Hermann stopped. The Countess appeared now to understand what he wanted; she seemed as if seeking for words to reply.

"It was a joke," she replied at last: "I assure you it was only a joke."

"There is no joking about the matter," replied Hermann angrily. "Remember Chaplitsky, whom you helped to win."

The Countess became visibly uneasy. Her features expressed strong emotion, but they quickly resumed their former immobility.

"Can you not name me these three winning cards?" continued Hermann.

The Countess remained silent; Hermann continued:

"For whom are you preserving your secret? For your grandsons? They are rich enough without it; they do not know the worth of money. Your cards would be of no use to a spendthrift. He who cannot preserve his paternal inheritance, will die in want, even though he had a demon at his service. I am not a man of that sort; I know the value of money. Your three cards will not be thrown away upon me. Come!" . . .

He paused and tremblingly awaited her reply. The Countess remained silent; Hermann fell upon his knees.

"If your heart has ever known the feeling of love," said he, "if you remember its rapture, if you have ever smiled at the cry of your newborn child, if any human feeling has ever entered into your breast, I entreat you by the feelings of a wife, a lover, a mother, by all that is most sacred in life, not to reject my prayer. Reveal to me your secret. Of what use is it to you? . . . May be it is connected with some terrible sin, with the loss of eternal salvation, with some bargain with the devil. . . . Reflect, — you are old; you have not long to live — I am ready to take your sins upon my soul. Only reveal to me your secret. Remember that the happiness of a man is in your hands, that not only I, but my children, and grandchildren will bless your memory and reverence you as a saint. . . ."

The old Countess answered not a word.

Hermann rose to his feet.

"You old hag!" he exclaimed, grinding his teeth, "then I will make you answer!"

With these words he drew a pistol from his pocket.

At the sight of the pistol, the Countess for the second time exhibited strong emotion. She shook her head and raised her hands as if to protect herself from the shot . . . then she fell backwards and remained motionless.

"Come, an end to this childish nonsense!" said Hermann, taking hold of her hand. "I ask you for the last time: will you tell me the names of your three cards, or will you not?"

The Countess made no reply. Hermann perceived that she was dead!

CHAPTER IV.

LIZAVETA IVANOVNA was sitting in her room, still in her ball dress, lost in deep thought. On returning home, she had hastily dismissed the chambermaid who very reluctantly came forward to assist her, saying that she would undress herself, and with a trembling heart had gone up to her own room, expecting to find Hermann there, but yet hoping not to find him. At the first glance she convinced herself that he was not there, and she thanked her fate for having prevented him keeping the appointment. She sat down without undressing, and began to recall to mind all the circumstances which in so short a time had carried her so far. It was not three weeks since the time when she first saw the young officer from the window — and yet she was already in correspondence with him, and he had succeeded in inducing her to grant him a nocturnal interview! She knew his name only through his having written it at the bottom of some of his letters; she had never spoken to him, had never heard his voice, and had never heard him spoken of until that evening. But, strange to say, that very evening at the ball, Tomsky, being piqued with the young Princess Pauline N——, who, contrary to her usual custom, did not flirt with him, wished to revenge himself by assuming an air of indifference: he therefore engaged Lizaveta Ivanovna and danced an endless mazurka with her. During the whole of the time he kept teasing her about her partiality for Engineer officers; he assured her that he knew far more than she imagined, and some of his jests were so happily aimed, that Lizaveta thought several times that her secret was known to him.

"From whom have you learnt all this?" she asked, smiling.

"From a friend of a person very well known to you," replied Tomsky, "from a very distinguished man."

"And who is this distinguished man?"

"His name is Hermann."

Lizaveta made no reply; but her hands and feet lost all sense of feeling.

"This Hermann," continued Tomsky, "is a man of romantic personality. He has the profile of a Napoleon, and the soul of a Mephistopheles. I believe that he has at least three crimes upon his conscience . . . How pale you have become!"

"I have a headache . . . But what did this Hermann — or whatever his name is — tell you?"

"Hermann is very much dissatisfied with his friend: he says that in his place he would act very differently . . . I even think that Hermann himself has designs upon you; at least, he listens very attentively to all that his friend has to say about you."

"And where has he seen me?"

"In church, perhaps; or on the parade — God alone knows where. It may have been in your room, while you were asleep, for there is nothing that he——"

Three ladies approaching him with the question: "*oubli ou regret?*"* interrupted the conversation, which had become so tantalizingly interesting to Lizaveta.

The lady chosen by Tomsky was the Princess Pauline herself. She succeeded in effecting a reconciliation with him during the numerous turns of the dance, after which he conducted her to her chair. On returning to his place, Tomsky thought no more either of Hermann or Lizaveta. She longed to renew the interrupted conversation, but the mazurka came to an end, and shortly afterwards the old Countess took her departure.

Tomsky's words were nothing more than the customary small talk of the dance, but they sank deep into the soul of the young dreamer. The portrait, sketched by Tomsky, coincided with the picture she had formed within her own mind, and thanks to the latest romances, the ordinary countenance of her admirer became invested with attributes capable of alarming her and fascinating her imagination at the same time. She was now sitting with her bare arms crossed and with her head, still adorned with flowers, sunk upon her uncovered bosom. Suddenly the door opened and Hermann entered. She shuddered.

"Where were you?" she asked in a terrified whisper.

"In the old Countess's bedroom," replied Hermann: "I have just left her. The Countess is dead."

"My God! What do you say?"

"And I am afraid," added Hermann, "that I am the cause of her death."

Lizaveta looked at him, and Tomsky's words found an echo in her soul: "This man has at least three crimes upon his conscience!" Hermann sat down by the window near her, and related all that had happened.

Lizaveta listened to him in terror. So all those passionate letters, those

* ["Forgetfulness or regret?": conventional words cloaking the identity of ladies requesting a dance; the man would choose a word and then dance with the corresponding lady.]

ardent desires, this bold obstinate pursuit—all this was not love! Money—that was what his soul yearned for! She could not satisfy his desire and make him happy! The poor girl had been nothing but the blind tool of a robber, of the murderer of her aged benefactress! . . . She wept bitter tears of agonized repentance. Hermann gazed at her in silence: his heart, too, was a prey to violent emotion, but neither the tears of the poor girl, nor the wonderful charm of her beauty, enhanced by her grief, could produce any impression upon his hardened soul. He felt no pricking of conscience at the thought of the dead old woman. One thing only grieved him: the irreparable loss of the secret from which he had expected to obtain great wealth.

"You are a monster!" said Lizaveta at last.

"I did not wish for her death," replied Hermann: "my pistol was not loaded."

Both remained silent.

The day began to dawn. Lizaveta extinguished her candle: a pale light illumined her room. She wiped her tear-stained eyes and raised them towards Hermann: he was sitting near the window, with his arms crossed and with a fierce frown upon his forehead. In this attitude he bore a striking resemblance to the portrait of Napoleon. This resemblance struck Lizaveta even.

"How shall I get you out of the house?" said she at last. "I thought of conducting you down the secret staircase, but in that case it would be necessary to go through the Countess's bedroom, and I am afraid."

"Tell me how to find this secret staircase—I will go alone."

Lizaveta arose, took from her drawer a key, handed it to Hermann and gave him the necessary instructions. Hermann pressed her cold, powerless hand, kissed her bowed head, and left the room.

He descended the winding staircase, and once more entered the Countess's bedroom. The dead old lady sat as if petrified; her face expressed profound tranquillity. Hermann stopped before her, and gazed long and earnestly at her, as if he wished to convince himself of the terrible reality; at last he entered the cabinet, felt behind the tapestry for the door, and then began to descend the dark staircase, filled with strange emotions. "Down this very staircase," thought he, "perhaps coming from the very same room, and at this very same hour sixty years ago, there may have glided, in an embroidered coat, with his hair dressed *à l'oiseau royal** and pressing to his heart his three-cornered hat, some young gallant who has long been mouldering in

---

* ["In the manner of the royal bird," the name of a contemporary hair style.]

the grave, but the heart of his aged mistress has only to-day ceased to beat. . . ."

At the bottom of the staircase Hermann found a door, which he opened with a key, and then traversed a corridor which conducted him into the street.

Chapter V.

Three days after the fatal night, at nine o'clock in the morning, Hermann repaired to the Convent of——, where the last honours were to be paid to the mortal remains of the old Countess. Although feeling no remorse, he could not altogether stifle the voice of conscience, which said to him: "You are the murderer of the old woman!" In spite of his entertaining very little religious belief, he was exceedingly superstitious; and believing that the dead Countess might exercise an evil influence on his life, he resolved to be present at her obsequies in order to implore her pardon.

The church was full. It was with difficulty that Hermann made his way through the crowd of people. The coffin was placed upon a rich catafalque beneath a velvet baldachin. The deceased Countess lay within it, with her hands crossed upon her breast, with a lace cap upon her head and dressed in a white satin robe. Around the catafalque stood the members of her household: the servants in black *caftans*, with armorial ribbons upon their shoulders, and candles in their hands; the relatives — children, grandchildren, and great-grandchildren — in deep mourning.

Nobody wept; tears would have been *une affectation*. The Countess was so old, that her death could have surprised nobody, and her relatives had long looked upon her as being out of the world. A famous preacher pronounced the funeral sermon. In simple and touching words he described the peaceful passing away of the righteous, who had passed long years in calm preparation for a Christian end. "The angel of death found her," said the orator, "engaged in pious meditation and waiting for the midnight bridegroom."

The service concluded amidst profound silence. The relatives went forward first to take farewell of the corpse. Then followed the numerous guests, who had come to render the last homage to her who for so many years had been a participator in their frivolous amusements. After these followed the members of the Countess's household. The last of these was an old woman of the same age as the deceased. Two young women led her forward by the hand. She had not strength enough to bow down to the ground — she merely shed a few tears and kissed the cold hand of her mistress.

Hermann now resolved to approach the coffin. He knelt down upon the cold stones and remained in that position for some minutes; at last he arose, as pale as the deceased Countess herself; he ascended the steps of the catafalque and bent over the corpse. . . . At that moment it seemed to him that the dead woman darted a mocking look at him and winked with one eye. Hermann started back, took a false step and fell to the ground. Several persons hurried forward and raised him up. At the same moment Lizaveta Ivanovna was borne fainting into the porch of the church. This episode disturbed for some minutes the solemnity of the gloomy ceremony. Among the congregation arose a deep murmur, and a tall thin chamberlain, a near relative of the deceased, whispered in the ear of an Englishman who was standing near him, that the young officer was a natural son of the Countess, to which the Englishman coldly replied: "Oh!"

During the whole of that day, Hermann was strangely excited. Repairing to an out-of-the-way restaurant to dine, he drank a great deal of wine, contrary to his usual custom, in the hope of deadening his inward agitation. But the wine only served to excite his imagination still more. On returning home, he threw himself upon his bed without undressing, and fell into a deep sleep.

When he woke up it was already night, and the moon was shining into the room. He looked at his watch: it was a quarter to three. Sleep had left him; he sat down upon his bed and thought of the funeral of the old Countess.

At that moment somebody in the street looked in at his window, and immediately passed on again. Hermann paid no attention to this incident. A few moments afterwards he heard the door of his ante-room open. Hermann thought that it was his orderly, drunk as usual, returning from some nocturnal expedition, but presently he heard footsteps that were unknown to him: somebody was walking softly over the floor in slippers. The door opened, and a woman dressed in white, entered the room. Hermann mistook her for his old nurse, and wondered what could bring her there at that hour of the night. But the white woman glided rapidly across the room and stood before him——and Hermann recognized the Countess!

"I have come to you against my wish," she said in a firm voice: "but I have been ordered to grant your request. Three, seven, ace, will win for you if played in succession, but only on these conditions: that you do not play more than one card in twenty-four hours, and that you never play again during the rest of your life. I forgive you my death, on condition that you marry my companion, Lizaveta Ivanovna."

With these words she turned round very quietly, walked with a shuffling gait towards the door and disappeared. Hermann heard the street-door open and shut, and again he saw someone look in at him through the window.

For a long time Hermann could not recover himself. He then rose up and entered the next room. His orderly was lying asleep upon the floor, and he had much difficulty in waking him. The orderly was drunk as usual, and no information could be obtained from him. The street-door was locked. Hermann returned to his room, lit his candle, and wrote down all the details of his vision.

Chapter VI.

Two fixed ideas can no more exist together in the moral world than two bodies can occupy one and the same place in the physical world. "Three, seven, ace" soon drove out of Hermann's mind the thought of the dead Countess. "Three, seven, ace" were perpetually running through his head and continually being repeated by his lips. If he saw a young girl, he would say: "How slender she is! quite like the three of hearts." If anybody asked: "What is the time?" he would reply: "Five minutes to seven." Every stout man that he saw reminded him of the ace. "Three, seven, ace" haunted him in his sleep, and assumed all possible shapes. The threes bloomed before him in the forms of magnificent flowers, the sevens were represented by Gothic portals, and the aces became transformed into gigantic spiders. One thought alone occupied his whole mind — to make a profitable use of the secret which he had purchased so dearly. He thought of applying for a furlough so as to travel abroad. He wanted to go to Paris and tempt fortune in some of the public gambling-houses that abounded there. Chance spared him all this trouble.

There was in Moscow a society of rich gamesters, presided over by the celebrated Chekalinsky, who had passed all his life at the card-table and had amassed millions, accepting bills of exchange for his winnings and paying his losses in ready money. His long experience secured for him the confidence of his companions, and his open house, his famous cook, and his agreeable and fascinating manners gained for him the respect of the public. He came to St. Petersburg. The young men of the capital flocked to his rooms, forgetting balls for cards, and preferring the emotions of faro to the seductions of flirting. Naroumoff conducted Hermann to Chekalinsky's residence.

They passed through a suite of magnificent rooms, filled with attentive domestics. The place was crowded. Generals and Privy Counsellors were playing at whist; young men were lolling carelessly upon the velvet-covered sofas, eating ices and smoking pipes. In the drawing-room, at the head of a long table, around which were assembled about a score of players, sat the master of the house keeping the bank. He was a man of about sixty years of age, of a very dignified appearance; his head was covered with silvery-white hair; his full, florid countenance expressed good-nature, and his eyes twinkled with a perpetual smile. Naroumoff introduced Hermann to him. Chekalinsky shook him by the hand in a friendly manner, requested him not to stand on ceremony, and then went on dealing.

The game occupied some time. On the table lay more than thirty cards. Chekalinsky paused after each throw, in order to give the players time to arrange their cards and note down their losses, listened politely to their requests, and more politely still, put straight the corners of cards that some player's hand had chanced to bend. At last the game was finished. Chekalinsky shuffled the cards and prepared to deal again.

"Will you allow me to take a card?" said Hermann, stretching out his hand from behind a stout gentleman who was punting.

Chekalinsky smiled and bowed silently, as a sign of acquiescence. Naroumoff laughingly congratulated Hermann on his abjuration of that abstention from cards which he had practised for so long a period, and wished him a lucky beginning.

"Stake!" said Hermann, writing some figures with chalk on the back of his card.

"How much?" asked the banker, contracting the muscles of his eyes; "excuse me, I cannot see quite clearly."

"Forty-seven thousand roubles," replied Hermann.

At these words every head in the room turned suddenly round, and all eyes were fixed upon Hermann.

"He has taken leave of his senses!" thought Naroumoff.

"Allow me to inform you," said Chekalinsky, with his eternal smile, "that you are playing very high; nobody here has ever staked more than two hundred and seventy-five roubles at once."

"Very well," replied Hermann; "but do you accept my card or not?"

Chekalinsky bowed in token of consent.

"I only wish to observe," said he, "that although I have the greatest confidence in my friends, I can only play against ready money. For my own part, I am quite convinced that your word is sufficient, but for the sake of the order of the game, and to facilitate the reckoning up, I must ask you to put the money on your card."

Hermann drew from his pocket a bank-note and handed it to Chekalinsky, who, after examining it in a cursory manner, placed it on Hermann's card.

He began to deal. On the right a nine turned up, and on the left a three.

"I have won!" said Hermann, showing his card.

A murmur of astonishment arose among the players. Chekalinsky frowned, but the smile quickly returned to his face.

"Do you wish me to settle with you?" he said to Hermann.

"If you please," replied the latter.

Chekalinsky drew from his pocket a number of bank-notes and paid at once. Hermann took up his money and left the table. Naroumoff could not recover from his astonishment. Hermann drank a glass of lemonade and returned home.

The next evening he again repaired to Chekalinsky's. The host was dealing. Hermann walked up to the table; the punters immediately made room for him. Chekalinsky greeted him with a gracious bow.

Hermann waited for the next deal, took a card and placed upon it his forty-seven thousand roubles, together with his winnings of the previous evening.

Chekalinsky began to deal. A knave turned up on the right, a seven on the left.

Hermann showed his seven.

There was a general exclamation. Chekalinsky was evidently ill at ease, but he counted out the ninety-four thousand roubles and handed them over to Hermann, who pocketed them in the coolest manner possible and immediately left the house.

The next evening Hermann appeared again at the table. Everyone was expecting him. The generals and Privy Counsellors left their whist in order to watch such extraordinary play. The young officers quitted their sofas, and even the servants crowded into the room. All pressed round Hermann. The other players left off punting, impatient to see how it would end. Hermann stood at the table and prepared to play alone against the pale, but still smiling Chekalinsky. Each opened a pack of cards. Chekalinsky shuffled. Hermann took a card and covered it with a pile of bank-notes. It was like a duel. Deep silence reigned around.

Chekalinsky began to deal; his hands trembled. On the right a queen turned up, and on the left an ace.

"Ace has won!" cried Hermann, showing his card.

"Your queen has lost," said Chekalinsky, politely.

Hermann started; instead of an ace, there lay before him the queen of spades! He could not believe his eyes, nor could he understand how he had made such a mistake.

At that moment it seemed to him that the queen of spades smiled ironically and winked her eye at him. He was struck by her remarkable resemblance. . . .

"The old Countess!" he exclaimed, seized with terror.

Chekalinsky gathered up his winnings. For some time, Hermann remained perfectly motionless. When at last he left the table, there was a general commotion in the room.

"Splendidly punted!" said the players. Chekalinsky shuffled the cards afresh, and the game went on as usual.

* * *

Hermann went out of his mind, and is now confined in room Number 17 of the Oboukhoff Hospital. He never answers any questions, but he constantly mutters with unusual rapidity: "Three, seven, ace! Three, seven, queen!"

Lizaveta Ivanovna has married a very amiable young man, a son of the former steward of the old Countess. He is in the service of the State somewhere, and is in receipt of a good income. Lizaveta is also supporting a poor relative.

Tomsky has been promoted to the rank of captain, and has become the husband of the Princess Pauline.

An Amateur Peasant Girl.

IN ONE OF our most distant governments was situated the domain of Ivan Petrovitch Berestoff. In his youth he had served in the Guards, but having quitted the service at the beginning of the year 1797, he repaired to his estate, and since that time he had not stirred away from it. He had married a poor but noble lady, who died in child-bed at a time when he was absent from home on a visit to one of the outlying fields of his domain. He soon found consolation in domestic occupations. He built a house on a plan of his own, established a cloth manufactory, made good use of his revenues, and began to consider himself the most sensible man in the whole country roundabout, and in this he was not contradicted by those of his neighbours who came to visit him with their families and their dogs. On week-days he wore a plush jacket, but on Sundays and holidays he appeared in a surtout of cloth that had been manufactured on his own premises. He himself kept an account of all his expenses, and he never read anything except the "Senate Gazette."

In general he was liked, although he was considered proud. There was only one person who was not on good terms with him, and that was Gregory Ivanovitch Mouromsky, his nearest neighbour. This latter was a genuine Russian noble of the old stamp. After having squandered in Moscow the greater part of his fortune, and having become a widower about the same time, he retired to his last remaining estate, where he continued to indulge in habits of extravagance, but of a new kind. He laid out an English garden, on which he expended nearly the whole of his remaining revenue. His grooms were dressed like English jockeys, his daughter had an English governess, and his fields were cultivated after the English method.

"But after the foreign manner Russian corn does not bear fruit," and in spite of a considerable reduction in his expenses, the revenues of Gregory Ivanovitch did not increase. He found means, even in the country, of contracting new debts. Nevertheless he was not considered a fool, for he was the first landowner in his government who conceived the idea of placing his estate under the safeguard of a council of tutelage* —

* [A loan institution requiring landed property as security.]

25

a proceeding which at that time was considered exceedingly complicated and venturesome. Of all those who censured him, Berestoff showed himself the most severe. Hatred of all innovation was a distinguishing trait in his character. He could not bring himself to speak calmly of the Anglomania of his neighbour, and he constantly found occasion to criticise him. If he showed his possessions to a guest, in reply to the praises bestowed upon him for his economical arrangements, he would say with a sly smile:

"Ah yes, it is not the same with me as with my neighbour Gregory Ivanovitch. What need have we to ruin ourselves in the English style, when we have enough to do to keep the wolf from the door in the Russian style?"

These, and similar sarcastic remarks, thanks to the zeal of obliging neighbours, did not fail to reach the ears of Gregory Ivanovitch greatly embellished. The Anglomaniac bore criticism as impatiently as our journalists. He became furious, and called his traducer a bear and a countryman.

Such were the relations between the two proprietors, when the son of Berestoff returned home to his father's estate. He had been educated at the University of ——, and was anxious to enter the military service, but to this his father would not give his consent. For the civil service the young man had not the slightest inclination, and as neither felt inclined to yield to the other, the young Alexei lived in the meantime like a nobleman, and allowed his moustache to grow at all events.[1]

Alexei was indeed a fine young fellow, and it would really have been a pity were his slender figure never to be set off to advantage by a military uniform, and were he to be compelled to spend his youth in bending over the papers of the chancery office, instead of bestriding a gallant steed. The neighbours, observing how he was always first in the chase, and always out of the beaten tracks, unanimously agreed that he would never make a useful official. The young ladies gazed after him, and sometimes cast stolen glances at him, but Alexei troubled himself very little about them, and they attributed this insensibility to some secret love affair. Indeed, there passed from hand to hand a copy of the address of one of his letters: "To Akoulina Petrovna Kourotchkin, in Moscow, opposite the Alexeivsky Monastery, in the house of the coppersmith Saveleff, with the request that she will forward this letter to A. N. R."

Those of my readers who have never lived in the country, cannot imagine how charming these provincial young ladies are! Brought up in

---

[1] It was formerly the custom in Russia for military men only to wear the moustache.

the pure air, under the shadow of the apple trees of their gardens, they derive their knowledge of the world and of life chiefly from books. Solitude, freedom, and reading develop very early within them sentiments and passions unknown to our town-bred beauties. For the young ladies of the country the sound of the post-bell is an event; a journey to the nearest town marks an epoch in their lives, and the visit of a guest leaves behind a long, and sometimes an eternal recollection. Of course everybody is at liberty to laugh at some of their peculiarities, but the jokes of a superficial observer cannot nullify their essential merits, the chief of which is that personality of character, that *individualité*, without which, in Jean Paul's* opinion, there can be no human greatness. In the capitals, women receive perhaps a better instruction, but intercourse with the world soon levels the character and makes their souls as uniform as their head-dresses. This is said neither by way of praise nor yet by way of censure, but "*nota nostra manet*,"† as one of the old commentators writes.

It can easily be imagined what impression Alexei would produce among the circle of our young ladies. He was the first who appeared before them gloomy and disenchanted, the first who spoke to them of lost happiness and of his blighted youth; in addition to which he wore a mourning ring engraved with a death's head. All this was something quite new in that distant government. The young ladies simply went out of their minds about him.

But not one of them felt so much interest in him as the daughter of our Anglomaniac Liza, or Betsy, as Gregory Ivanovitch usually called her. As their parents did not visit each other, she had not yet seen Alexei, even when he had become the sole topic of conversation among all the young ladies of the neighbourhood. She was seventeen years of age. Dark eyes illuminated her swarthy and exceedingly pleasant countenance. She was an only child, and consequently she was perfectly spoiled. Her wantonness and continual pranks delighted her father and filled with despair the heart of Miss Jackson, her governess, an affected old maid of forty, who powdered her face and darkened her eyebrows, read through "Pamela"[1] twice a year, for which she received two thousand roubles, and felt almost bored to death in this barbarous Russia of ours.

Liza was waited upon by Nastia, who, although somewhat older, was

* [German author (surname Richter), 1763–1825.]
† ["Our stamp remains."]
[1] A novel written by Samuel Richardson, and first published in 1740.

quite as giddy as her mistress. Liza was very fond of her, revealed to her all her secrets, and planned pranks together with her; in a word, Nastia was a far more important person in the village of Priloutchina, than the trusted confidante in a French tragedy.

"Will you allow me to go out to-day on a visit?" said Nastia one morning, as she was dressing her mistress.

"Very well; but where are you going to?"

"To Tougilovo, to the Berestoffs. The wife of their cook is going to celebrate her name-day to-day, and she came over yesterday to invite us to dinner."

"That's curious," said Liza: "the masters are at daggers drawn, but the servants fête each other."

"What have the masters to do with us?" replied Nastia. "Besides, I belong to you, and not to your papa. You have not had any quarrel with young Berestoff; let the old ones quarrel and fight, if it gives them any pleasure."

"Try and see Alexei Berestoff, Nastia, and then tell me what he looks like and what sort of a person he is."

Nastia promised to do so, and all day long Liza waited with impatience for her return. In the evening Nastia made her appearance.

"Well, Lizaveta Gregorievna," said she, on entering the room, "I have seen young Berestoff, and I had ample opportunity for taking a good look at him, for we have been together all day."

"How did that happen? Tell me about it, tell me everything about it."

"Very well. We set out, I, Anissia Egorovna, Nenila, Dounka. . . ."

"Yes, yes, I know. And then?"

"With your leave, I will tell you everything in detail. We arrived just in time for dinner. The room was full of people. The Kolbinskys were there, as well as the Zakharevskys, the Khloupinskys, the bailiff's wife and her daughters. . . ."

"Well, and Berestoff?"

"Wait a moment. We sat down to table; the bailiff's wife had the place of honour. I sat next to her . . . the daughters pouted and didn't like it, but I didn't care about them. . . ."

"Good heavens, Nastia, how tiresome you are with your never-ending details!"

"How impatient you are! Well, we rose from the table . . . we had been sitting down for three hours, and the dinner was excellent: pastry, blanc-manges, blue, red and striped. . . . Well, we left the table and went into the garden to have a game at catching one another, and it was then that the young lord made his appearance."

"Well, and is it true that he is so very handsome?"

"Exceedingly handsome: tall, well-built, and with red cheeks. . . ."

"Really? And I was under the impression that he was fair. Well, and how did he seem to you? Sad, thoughtful?"

"Nothing of the kind! I have never in my life seen such a frolicsome person. He wanted to join in the game with us."

"Join in the game with you? Impossible!"

"Not all impossible. And what else do you think he wanted to do? To kiss us all round!"

"With your permission, Nastia, you are talking nonsense."

"With your permission, I am not talking nonsense. I had the greatest trouble in the world to get away from him. He spent the whole day along with us."

"But they say that he is in love, and hasn't eyes for anybody."

"I don't know anything about that, but I know that he looked at me a good deal, and so he did at Tania, the bailiff's daughter, and at Pasha[1] Kolbinsky also. But it cannot be said that he offended anybody — he is so very agreeable."

"That is extraordinary! And what do they say about him in the house?"

"They say that he is an excellent master — so kind, so cheerful. They have only one fault to find with him: he is too fond of running after the young girls. But for my part, I don't think that is a very great fault: he will grow steady with age."

"How I should like to see him!" said Liza, with a sigh.

"What is there to hinder you from doing so? Tougilovo is not far from us — only about three versts. Go and take a walk in that direction, or a ride on horseback, and you will assuredly meet him. He goes out early every morning with his gun."

"No, no, that would not do. He might think that I was running after him. Besides, our fathers are not on good terms, so that I cannot make his acquaintance. . . . Ah! Nastia, do you know what I'll do? I will dress myself up as a peasant girl!"

"Exactly! Put on a coarse chemise and a *sarafan*, and then go boldly to Tougilovo; I will answer for it that Berestoff will not pass by without taking notice of you."

"And I know how to imitate the style of speech of the peasants about here. Ah, Nastia! my dear Nastia! what an excellent idea!"

And Liza went to bed, firmly resolved on putting her plan into execution.

---

[1] Diminutive of Praskovia.

The next morning she began to prepare for the accomplishment of her scheme. She sent to the bazaar and bought some coarse linen, some blue nankeen and some copper buttons, and with the help of Nastia she cut out for herself a chemise and *sarafan*. She then set all the female servants to work to do the necessary sewing, so that by the evening everything was ready. Liza tried on the new costume, and as she stood before the mirror, she confessed to herself that she had never looked so charming. Then she practised her part. As she walked she made a low bow, and then tossed her head several times, after the manner of a china cat, spoke in the peasants' dialect, smiled behind her sleeve, and did everything to Nastia's complete satisfaction. One thing only proved irksome to her: she tried to walk barefooted across the courtyard, but the turf pricked her tender feet, and she found the stones and gravel unbearable. Nastia immediately came to her assistance. She took the measurement of Liza's foot, ran to the fields to find Trophim the shepherd, and ordered him to make a pair of bast shoes of the same measurement.

The next morning, almost before it was dawn, Liza was already awake. Everybody in the house was still asleep. Nastia went to the gate to wait for the shepherd. The sound of a horn was heard, and the village flock defiled past the manor-house. Trophim, on passing by Nastia, gave her a small pair of coloured bast shoes, and received from her a half-rouble in exchange. Liza quietly dressed herself in the peasant's costume, whispered her instructions to Nastia with reference to Miss Jackson, descended the back staircase and made her way through the garden into the field beyond.

The eastern sky was all aglow, and the golden lines of clouds seemed to be awaiting the sun, like courtiers await their monarch. The bright sky, the freshness of the morning, the dew, the light breeze, and the singing of the birds filled the heart of Liza with childish joy. The fear of meeting some acquaintance seemed to give her wings, for she flew rather than walked. But as she approached the wood which formed the boundary of her father's estate, she slackened her pace. Here she resolved to wait for Alexei. Her heart beat violently, she knew not why; but is not the fear which accompanies our youthful escapades that which constitutes their greatest charm? Liza advanced into the depth of the wood. The deep murmur of the waving branches seemed to welcome the young girl. Her gaiety vanished. Little by little she abandoned herself to sweet reveries. She thought — but who can say exactly what a young lady of seventeen thinks of, alone in a wood, at six o'clock of a spring morning? And so she walked musingly along the pathway, which was shaded on both sides by tall trees, when suddenly a magnificent hunting dog came barking and bounding towards her. Liza became alarmed and cried out. But at the same moment a voice called out: "*Tout beau, Sbogar, ici!*"* . . . and a young hunter emerged from behind a clump of bushes.

"Don't be afraid, my dear," said he to Liza: "my dog does not bite."

Liza had already recovered from her alarm, and she immediately took advantage of her opportunity.

"But, sir," said she, assuming a half-frightened, half-bashful expression, "I am so afraid; he looks so fierce — he might fly at me again."

Alexei — for the reader has already recognized him — gazed fixedly at the young peasant-girl.

"I will accompany you if you are afraid," said he to her: "will you allow me to walk along with you?"

"Who is to hinder you?" replied Liza. "Wills are free, and the road is open to everybody."

"Where do you come from?"

"From Priloutchina; I am the daughter of Vassili the blacksmith, and I am going to gather mushrooms." (Liza carried a basket on her arm.) "And you, sir? From Tougilovo, I have no doubt."

"Exactly so," replied Alexei: "I am the young master's valet-de-chambre."

Alexei wanted to put himself on an equality with her, but Liza looked at him and began to smile.

"That is a fib," said she: "I am not such a fool as you may think. I see very well that you are the young master himself."

"Why do you think so?"

"I think so for a great many reasons."

"But——"

"As if it were not possible to distinguish the master from the servant! You are not dressed like a servant, you do not speak like one, and you address your dog in a different way to us."

Liza began to please Alexei more and more. As he was not accustomed to standing upon ceremony with peasant girls, he wanted to embrace her; but Liza drew back from him, and suddenly assumed such a cold and severe look, that Alexei, although much amused, did not venture to renew the attempt.

"If you wish that we should remain good friends," said she with dignity, "be good enough not to forget yourself."

"Who taught you such wisdom?" asked Alexei, bursting into a laugh.

* ["Good boy, Sbogar, come here!"]

"Can it be my friend Nastenka,[1] the chambermaid to your young mistress? See by what paths enlightenment becomes diffused!"

Liza felt that she had stepped out of her rôle, and she immediately recovered herself.

"Do you think," said she, "that I have never been to the manor-house? Don't alarm yourself; I have seen and heard a great many things. . . . But," continued she, "if I talk to you, I shall not gather my mushrooms. Go your way, sir, and I will go mine. Pray excuse me."

And she was about to move off, but Alexei seized hold of her hand.

"What is your name, my dear?"

"Akoulina," replied Liza, endeavouring to disengage her fingers from his grasp: "but let me go, sir; it is time for me to return home."

"Well, my friend Akoulina, I will certainly pay a visit to your father, Vassili the blacksmith."

"What do you say?" replied Liza quickly: "for Heaven's sake, don't think of doing such a thing! If it were known at home that I had been talking to a gentleman alone in the wood, I should fare very badly, — my father, Vassili the blacksmith, would beat me to death."

"But I really must see you again."

"Well, then, I will come here again some time to gather mushrooms."

"When?"

"Well, to-morrow, if you wish it."

"My dear Akoulina, I would kiss you, but I dare not. . . . To-morrow, then, at the same time, isn't that so?"

"Yes, yes!"

"And you will not deceive me?"

"I will not deceive you."

"Swear it."

"Well, then, I swear by Holy Friday that I will come."

The young people separated. Liza emerged from the wood, crossed the field, stole into the garden and hastened to the place where Nastia awaited her. There she changed her costume, replying absently to the questions of her impatient confidante, and then she repaired to the parlour. The cloth was laid, the breakfast was ready, and Miss Jackson, already powdered and laced up, so that she looked like a wine-glass, was cutting thin slices of bread and butter.

Her father praised her for her early walk.

"There is nothing so healthy," said he, "as getting up at daybreak." Then he cited several instances of human longevity, which he had

[1] Diminutive of Nastia.

derived from the English journals, and observed that all persons who had lived to be upwards of a hundred, abstained from brandy and rose at daybreak, winter and summer.

Liza did not listen to him. In her thoughts she was going over all the circumstances of the meeting of that morning, all the conversation of Akoulina with the young hunter, and her conscience began to torment her. In vain did she try to persuade herself that their conversation had not gone beyond the bounds of propriety, and that the frolic would be followed by no serious consequences—her conscience spoke louder than her reason. The promise given for the following day troubled her more than anything else, and she almost felt resolved not to keep her solemn oath. But then, might not Alexei, after waiting for her in vain, make his way to the village and search out the daughter of Vassili the blacksmith, the veritable Akoulina—a fat, pock-marked peasant girl—and so discover the prank she had played upon him? This thought frightened Liza, and she resolved to repair again to the little wood the next morning in the same disguise as at first.

On his side, Alexei was in an ecstasy of delight. All day long he thought of his new acquaintance; and in his dreams at night the form of the dark-skinned beauty appeared before him. The morning had scarcely begun to dawn, when he was already dressed. Without giving himself time to load his gun, he set out for the fields with his faithful Sbogar, and hastened to the place of the promised rendezvous. A half hour of intolerable waiting passed by; at last he caught a glimpse of a blue *sarafan* between the bushes, and he rushed forward to meet his charming Akoulina. She smiled at the ecstatic nature of his thanks, but Alexei immediately observed upon her face traces of sadness and uneasiness. He wished to know the cause. Liza confessed to him that her act seemed to her very frivolous, that she repented of it, that this time she did not wish to break her promised word, but that this meeting would be the last, and she therefore entreated him to break off an acquaintanceship which could not lead to any good.

All this, of course, was expressed in the language of a peasant; but such thoughts and sentiments, so unusual in a simple girl of the lower class, struck Alexei with astonishment. He employed all his eloquence to divert Akoulina from her purpose; he assured her that his intentions were honourable, promised her that he would never give her cause to repent, that he would obey her in everything, and earnestly entreated her not to deprive him of the joy of seeing her alone, if only once a day, or even only twice a week. He spoke the language of true passion, and at that moment he was really in love. Liza listened to him in silence.

"Give me your word," said she at last, "that you will never come to the village in search of me, and that you will never seek a meeting with me except those that I shall appoint myself."

Alexei swore by Holy Friday, but she stopped him with a smile.

"I do not want you to swear," said she; "your mere word is sufficient."

After that they began to converse together in a friendly manner, strolling about the wood, until Liza said to him:

"It is time for me to return home."

They separated, and when Alexei was left alone, he could not understand how, in two interviews, a simple peasant girl had succeeded in acquiring such influence over him. His relations with Akoulina had for him all the charm of novelty, and although the injunctions of the strange young girl appeared to him to be very severe, the thought of breaking his word never once entered his mind. The fact was that Alexei, in spite of his fatal ring, his mysterious correspondence and his gloomy disenchantment, was a good and impulsive young fellow, with a pure heart capable of enjoying the pleasures of innocence.

Were I to listen to my own wishes only, I would here enter into a minute description of the interviews of the young people, of their growing passion for each other, their confidences, occupations and conversations; but I know that the greater part of my readers would not share my satisfaction. Such details are usually considered tedious and uninteresting, and therefore I will omit them, merely observing, that before two months had elapsed, Alexei was already hopelessly in love, and Liza equally so, though less demonstrative in revealing the fact. Both were happy in the present and troubled themselves little about the future.

The thought of indissoluble ties frequently passed through their minds, but never had they spoken to each other about the matter. The reason was plain: Alexei, however much attached he might be to his lovely Akoulina, could not forget the distance that separated him from the poor peasant girl; while Liza, knowing the hatred that existed between their parents, did not dare to hope for a mutual reconciliation. Moreover, her self-love was stimulated in secret by the obscure and romantic hope of seeing at last the proprietor of Tougilovo at the feet of the blacksmith's daughter of Priloutchina. All at once an important event occurred which threatened to interrupt their mutual relations.

One bright cold morning — such a morning as is very common during our Russian autumn — Ivan Petrovitch Berestoff went out for a ride on horseback, taking with him three pairs of hunting dogs, a game-keeper and several stable-boys with clappers. At the same time, Gregory

Ivanovitch Mouromsky, seduced by the beautiful weather, ordered his bob-tailed mare to be saddled, and started out to visit his domains cultivated in the English style. On approaching the wood, he perceived his neighbour, sitting proudly on his horse, in his cloak lined with fox-skin, waiting for a hare which his followers, with loud cries and the rattling of their clappers, had started out of a thicket. If Gregory Ivanovitch had foreseen this meeting, he would certainly have proceeded in another direction, but he came upon Berestoff so unexpectedly, that he suddenly found himself no farther than the distance of a pistol-shot away from him. There was no help for it: Mouromsky, like a civilized European, rode forward towards his adversary and politely saluted him. Berestoff returned the salute with the characteristic grace of a chained bear, who salutes the public in obedience to the order of his master.

At that moment the hare darted out of the wood and started off across the field. Berestoff and the gamekeeper raised a loud shout, let the dogs loose, and then galloped off in pursuit. Mouromsky's horse, not being accustomed to hunting, took fright and bolted. Mouromsky, who prided himself on being a good horseman, gave it full rein, and inwardly rejoiced at the incident which delivered him from a disagreeable companion. But the horse, reaching a ravine which it had not previously noticed, suddenly sprang to one side, and Mouromsky was thrown from the saddle. Striking the frozen ground with considerable force, he lay there cursing his bob-tailed mare, which, as if recovering from its fright, had suddenly come to a standstill as soon as it felt that it was without a rider.

Ivan Petrovitch hastened towards him and inquired if he had injured himself. In the meantime the gamekeeper had secured the guilty horse, which he now led forward by the bridle. He helped Mouromsky into the saddle, and Berestoff invited him to his house. Mouromsky could not refuse the invitation, for he felt indebted to him; and so Berestoff returned home, covered with glory for having hunted down a hare and for bringing with him his adversary wounded and almost a prisoner of war.

The two neighbours took breakfast together and conversed with each other in a very friendly manner. Mouromsky requested Berestoff to lend him a *droshky*, for he was obliged to confess that, owing to his bruises, he was not in a condition to return home on horseback. Berestoff conducted him to the steps, and Mouromsky did not take leave of him until he had obtained a promise from him that he would come the next day in company with Alexei Ivanovitch, and dine in a friendly way at Priloutchina. In this way was a deeply-rooted enmity of long standing apparently brought to an end by the skittishness of a bob-tailed mare.

Liza ran forward to meet Gregory Ivanovitch.

"What does this mean, papa?" said she with astonishment. "Why are you walking lame? Where is your horse? Whose is this *droshky?*"

"You will never guess, my dear," replied Gregory Ivanovitch; and then he related to her everything that had happened.

Liza could not believe her ears. Without giving her time to collect herself, Gregory Ivanovitch then went on to inform her that the two Berestoffs—father and son—would dine with them on the following day.

"What do you say?" she exclaimed, turning pale. "The Berestoffs, father and son, will dine with us to-morrow! No, papa, you can do as you please, but I shall not show myself."

"Have you taken leave of your senses?" replied her father. "Since when have you been so bashful? Or do you cherish an hereditary hatred towards him like a heroine of romance? Enough, do not act the fool."

"No, papa, not for anything in the world, not for any treasure would I appear before the Berestoffs."

Gregory Ivanovitch shrugged his shoulders, and did not dispute with her any further, for he knew that by contradiction he would obtain nothing from her. He therefore went to rest himself after his remarkable ride.

Lizaveta Gregorievna repaired to her room and summoned Nastia. They both conversed together for a long time about the impending visit. What would Alexei think if, in the well-bred young lady, he recognized his Akoulina? What opinion would he have of her conduct, of her manners, of her good sense? On the other hand, Liza wished very much to see what impression would be produced upon him by a meeting so unexpected. . . . Suddenly an idea flashed through her mind. She communicated it to Nastia; both felt delighted with it, and they resolved to carry it into effect.

The next day at breakfast, Gregory Ivanovitch asked his daughter if she still intended to avoid the Berestoffs.

"Papa," replied Liza, "I will receive them if you wish it, but on one condition, and that is, that however I may appear before them, or whatever I may do, you will not be angry with me, or show the least sign of astonishment or displeasure."

"Some new freak!" said Gregory Ivanovitch, laughing. "Very well, very well, I agree; do what you like, my dark-eyed romp."

With these words he kissed her on the forehead, and Liza ran off to put her plan into execution.

At two o'clock precisely, a Russian calèche, drawn by six horses, entered the courtyard and rounded the lawn. The elder Berestoff mounted the steps with the assistance of two lackeys in the Mouromsky livery. His son came after him on horseback, and both entered together into the dining-room, where the table was already laid. Mouromsky received his neighbours in the most gracious manner, proposed to them to inspect his garden and park before dinner, and conducted them along paths carefully kept and gravelled. The elder Berestoff inwardly deplored the time and labour wasted in such useless fancies, but he held his tongue out of politeness. His son shared neither the disapprobation of the economical landowner, nor the enthusiasm of the vain-glorious Anglomaniac, but waited with impatience for the appearance of his host's daughter, of whom he had heard a great deal; and although his heart, as we know, was already engaged, youthful beauty always had a claim upon his imagination.

Returning to the parlour, they all three sat down; and while the old men recalled their young days, and related anecdotes of their respective careers, Alexei considered in his mind what rôle he should play in the presence of Liza. He came to the conclusion that an air of cold indifference would be the most becoming under the circumstances, and he prepared to act accordingly. The door opened; he turned his head with such indifference, with such haughty carelessness, that the heart of the most inveterate coquette would inevitably have shuddered. Unfortunately, instead of Liza, it was old Miss Jackson, who, painted and bedecked, entered the room with downcast eyes and with a low bow, so that Alexei's dignified military salute was lost upon her. He had not succeeded in recovering from his confusion, when the door opened again, and this time it was Liza herself who entered.

All rose; her father was just beginning to introduce his guests, when suddenly he stopped short and bit his lips. . . . Liza, his dark-complexioned Liza, was painted white up to the ears, and was more bedizened than even Miss Jackson herself; false curls, much lighter than her own hair, covered her head like the perruque of Louis the Fourteenth; her sleeves à l'imbécile* stood out like the hooped skirts of Madame de Pompadour; her figure was pinched in like the letter X, and all her mother's jewels, which had not yet found their way to the pawnbroker's, shone upon her fingers, her neck and in her ears.

* [Narrow sleeves with shoulder puffs.]

Alexei could not possibly recognize his Akoulina in the grotesque and brilliant young lady. His father kissed her hand, and he followed his example, though much against his will; when he touched her little white fingers, it seemed to him that they trembled. In the meantime he succeeded in catching a glimpse of her little foot, intentionally advanced and set off to advantage by the most coquettish shoe imaginable. This reconciled him somewhat to the rest of her toilette. As for the paint and powder, it must be confessed that, in the simplicity of his heart, he had not noticed them at the first glance, and afterwards had no suspicion of them. Gregory Ivanovitch remembered his promise, and endeavoured not to show any astonishment; but his daughter's freak seemed to him so amusing, that he could scarcely contain himself. But the person who felt no inclination to laugh was the affected English governess. She had a shrewd suspicion that the paint and powder had been extracted from her chest of drawers, and the deep flush of anger was distinctly visible beneath the artificial whiteness of her face. She darted angry glances at the young madcap, who, reserving her explanations for another time, pretended that she did not notice them.

They sat down to table. Alexei continued to play his rôle of assumed indifference and absence of mind. Liza put on an air of affectation, spoke through her teeth, and only in French. Her father kept constantly looking at her, not understanding her aim, but finding it all exceedingly amusing. The English governess fumed with rage and said not a word. Ivan Petrovitch alone seemed at home: he ate like two, drank heavily, laughed at his own jokes, and grew more talkative and hilarious at every moment.

At last they all rose up from the table; the guests took their departure, and Gregory Ivanovitch gave free vent to his laughter and to his interrogations.

"What put the idea into your head of acting the fool like that with them?" he said to Liza. "But do you know what? The paint suits you admirably. I do not wish to fathom the mysteries of a lady's toilette, but if I were in your place, I would very soon begin to paint; not too much, of course, but just a little."

Liza was enchanted with the success of her stratagem. She embraced her father, promised him that she would consider his advice, and then hastened to conciliate the indignant Miss Jackson, who, with great reluctance consented to open the door and listen to her explanations. Liza was ashamed to appear before strangers with her dark complexion; she had not dared to ask. . . . she felt sure that dear, good Miss Jackson would pardon her, etc., etc. Miss Jackson, feeling convinced that Liza had not wished to make her a laughing-stock by imitating her, calmed down, kissed her, and as a token of reconciliation, made her a present of a small pot of English paint, which Liza accepted with every appearance of sincere gratitude.

The reader will readily imagine that Liza lost no time in repairing to the rendezvous in the little wood the next morning.

"You were at our master's yesterday," she said at once to Alexei: "what do you think of our young mistress?"

Alexei replied that he had not observed her.

"That's a pity!" replied Liza.

"Why so?" asked Alexei.

"Because I wanted to ask you if it is true what they say——"

"What do they say?"

"Is it true, as they say, that I am very much like her?"

"What nonsense! She is a perfect monstrosity compared with you."

"Oh, sir, it is very wrong of you to speak like that. Our young mistress is so fair and so stylish! How could I be compared with her!"

Alexei vowed to her that she was more beautiful than all the fair young ladies in creation, and in order to pacify her completely, he began to describe her mistress in such comical terms, that Liza laughed heartily.

"But," said she with a sigh, "even though our young mistress may be ridiculous, I am but a poor ignorant thing in comparison with her."

"Oh!" said Alexei; "is that anything to break your heart about? If you wish it, I will soon teach you to read and write."

"Yes, indeed," said Liza, "why should I not try?"

"Very well, my dear; we will commence at once."

They sat down. Alexei drew from his pocket a pencil and note-book, and Akoulina learnt the alphabet with astonishing rapidity. Alexei could not sufficiently admire her intelligence. The following morning she wished to try to write. At first the pencil refused to obey her, but after a few minutes she was able to trace the letters with tolerable accuracy.

"It is really wonderful!" said Alexei. "Our method certainly produces quicker results than the Lancaster system."[1]

And indeed, at the third lesson Akoulina began to spell through "Nathalie the Boyard's Daughter,"* interrupting her reading by observations which really filled Alexei with astonishment, and she filled a whole sheet of paper with aphorisms drawn from the same story.

---

[1] An allusion to the system of education introduced into England by Joseph Lancaster at the commencement of the present [19th] century.

* [A story by Karamzin.]

A week went by, and a correspondence was established between them. Their letter-box was the hollow of an old oak-tree, and Nastia acted as their messenger. Thither Alexei carried his letters written in a bold round hand, and there he found on plain blue paper the delicately-traced strokes of his beloved. Akoulina perceptibly began to acquire an elegant style of expression, and her mental faculties commenced to develop themselves with astonishing rapidity.

Meanwhile, the recently-formed acquaintance between Ivan Petrovitch Berestoff and Gregory Ivanovitch Mouromsky soon became transformed into a sincere friendship, under the following circumstances. Mouromsky frequently reflected that, on the death of Ivan Petrovitch, all his possessions would pass into the hands of Alexei Ivanovitch, in which case the latter would be one of the wealthiest landed proprietors in the government, and there would be nothing to hinder him from marrying Liza. The elder Berestoff, on his side, although recognizing in his neighbour a certain extravagance (or, as he termed it, English folly), was perfectly ready to admit that he possessed many excellent qualities, as for example, his rare tact. Gregory Ivanovitch was closely related to Count Pronsky, a man of distinction and of great influence. The Count could be of great service to Alexei, and Mouromsky (so thought Ivan Petrovitch) would doubtless rejoice to see his daughter marry so advantageously. By dint of constantly dwelling upon this idea, the two old men came at last to communicate their thoughts to one another. They embraced each other, both promised to do their best to arrange the matter, and they immediately set to work, each on his own side. Mouromsky foresaw that he would have some difficulty in persuading his Betsy to become more intimately acquainted with Alexei, whom she had not seen since the memorable dinner. It seemed to him that they had not been particularly well pleased with each other; at least Alexei had not paid any further visits to Priloutchina, and Liza had retired to her room every time that Ivan Petrovitch had honoured them with a visit.

"But," thought Gregory Ivanovitch, "if Alexei came to see us every day, Betsy could not help falling in love with him. That is the natural order of things. Time will settle everything."

Ivan Petrovitch was no less uneasy about the success of his designs. That same evening he summoned his son into his cabinet, lit his pipe, and, after a long pause, said:

"Well, Alesha,[1] what do you think about doing? You have not said

---

[1] Diminutive of Alexei (Alexis).

anything for a long time about the military service. Or has the Hussar uniform lost its charm for you?"

"No, father," replied Alexei respectfully; "but I see that you do not like the idea of my entering the Hussars, and it is my duty to obey you."

"Good," replied Ivan Petrovitch; "I see that you are an obedient son; that is very consoling to me. . . . On my side, I do not wish to compel you; I do not want to force you to enter . . . at once . . . into the civil service, but, in the meanwhile, I intend you to get married."

"To whom, father?" asked Alexei in astonishment.

"To Lizaveta Gregorievna Mouromsky," replied Ivan Petrovitch. "She is a charming bride, is she not?"

"Father, I have not thought of marriage yet."

"You have not thought of it, and therefore I have thought of it for you."

"As you please, but I do not care for Liza Mouromsky in the least."

"You will get to like her afterwards. Love comes with time."

"I do not feel capable of making her happy."

"Do not distress yourself about making her happy. What? Is this how you respect your father's wish? Very well!"

"As you please. I do not wish to marry, and I will not marry."

"You will marry, or I will curse you; and as for my possessions, as true as God is holy, I will sell them and squander the money, and not leave you a farthing. I will give you three days to think about the matter; and in the meantime, don't show yourself in my sight."

Alexei knew that when his father once took an idea into his head, a nail even would not drive it out, as Taras Skotinin[1] says in the comedy. But Alexei took after his father, and was just as head-strong as he was. He went to his room and began to reflect upon the limits of paternal authority. Then his thoughts reverted to Lizaveta Gregorievna, to his father's solemn vow to make him a beggar, and last of all to Akoulina. For the first time he saw clearly that he was passionately in love with her; the romantic idea of marrying a peasant girl and of living by the labour of their hands came into his head, and the more he thought of such a decisive step, the more reasonable did it seem to him. For some time the interviews in the wood had ceased on account of the rainy weather. He wrote to Akoulina a letter in his most legible handwriting, informing her of the misfortune that threatened them, and offering her his hand. He took the letter at once to the post-office in the wood, and then went to bed, well satisfied with himself.

The next day Alexei, still firm in his resolution, rode over early in the

---

[1] A character in "Nedorosl," a comedy by Denis Von Vizin.

morning to visit Mouromsky, in order to explain matters frankly to him. He hoped to excite his generosity and win him over to his side.

"Is Gregory Ivanovitch at home?" asked he, stopping his horse in front of the steps of the Priloutchina mansion.

"No," replied the servant; "Gregory Ivanovitch rode out early this morning, and has not yet returned."

"How annoying!" thought Alexei. . . . "Is Lizaveta Gregorievna at home, then?" he asked.

"Yes, sir."

Alexei sprang from his horse, gave the reins to the lackey, and entered without being announced.

"Everything is now going to be decided," thought he, directing his steps towards the parlour: "I will explain everything to Lizaveta herself." He entered . . . and then stood still as if petrified! Liza . . . no . . . Akoulina, dear, dark-haired Akoulina, no longer in a *sarafan*, but in a white morning robe, was sitting in front of the window, reading his letter; she was so occupied that she had not heard him enter.

Alexei could not restrain an exclamation of joy. Liza started, raised her head, uttered a cry, and wished to fly from the room. But he threw himself before her and held her back.

"Akoulina! Akoulina!"

Liza endeavoured to liberate herself from his grasp.

"*Mais laissez-moi donc, Monsieur! . . . Mais êtes-vous fou?*"* she said, twisting herself round.

"Akoulina! my dear Akoulina!" he repeated, kissing her hand.

Miss Jackson, a witness of this scene, knew not what to think of it. At that moment the door opened, and Gregory Ivanovitch entered the room.

"Ah! ah!" said Mouromsky; "but it seems that you have already arranged matters between you."

The reader will spare me the unnecessary obligation of describing the dénouement.

* ["Let me go, sir! . . . Are you mad?"]

The Shot.

CHAPTER I.

WE WERE STATIONED in the little town of N——. The life of an officer in the army is well known. In the morning, drill and the riding-school; dinner with the Colonel or at a Jewish restaurant; in the evening, punch and cards. In N—— there was not one open house, not a single marriageable girl. We used to meet in each other's rooms, where, except our uniforms, we never saw anything.

One civilian only was admitted into our society. He was about thirty-five years of age, and therefore we looked upon him as an old fellow. His experience gave him great advantage over us, and his habitual taciturnity, stern disposition and caustic tongue produced a deep impression upon our young minds. Some mystery surrounded his existence; he had the appearance of a Russian, although his name was a foreign one. He had formerly served in the Hussars, and with distinction. Nobody knew the cause that had induced him to retire from the service and settle in a wretched little village, where he lived poorly and, at the same time, extravagantly. He always went on foot, and constantly wore a shabby black overcoat, but the officers of our regiment were ever welcome at his table. His dinners, it is true, never consisted of more than two or three dishes, prepared by a retired soldier, but the champagne flowed like water. Nobody knew what his circumstances were, or what his income was, and nobody dared to question him about them. He had a collection of books, consisting chiefly of works on military matters and a few novels. He willingly lent them to us to read, and never asked for them back; on the other hand, he never returned to the owner the books that were lent to him. His principal amusement was shooting with a pistol. The walls of his room were riddled with bullets, and were as full of holes as a honey-comb. A rich collection of pistols was the only luxury in the humble cottage where he lived. The skill which he had acquired with his favourite weapon was simply incredible; and if he had offered to shoot a pear off somebody's forage-cap, not a man in our regiment would have hesitated to place the object upon his head.

Our conversation often turned upon duels. Silvio — so I will call him — never joined in it. When asked if he had ever fought, he drily replied that he had; but he entered into no particulars, and it was evident that such questions were not to his liking. We came to the conclusion that he had upon his conscience the memory of some unhappy victim of his terrible skill. Moreover, it never entered into the head of any of us to suspect him of anything like cowardice. There are persons whose mere look is sufficient to repel such a suspicion. But an unexpected incident occurred which astounded us all.

One day, about ten of our officers dined with Silvio. They drank as usual, that is to say, a great deal. After dinner we asked our host to hold the bank for a game at faro. For a long time he refused, for he hardly ever played, but at last he ordered cards to be brought, placed half a hundred ducats upon the table, and sat down to deal. We took our places round him, and the play began. It was Silvio's custom to preserve a complete silence when playing. He never disputed, and never entered into explanations. If the punter made a mistake in calculating, he immediately paid him the difference or noted down the surplus. We were acquainted with this habit of his, and we always allowed him to have his own way; but among us on this occasion was an officer who had only recently been transferred to our regiment. During the course of the game, this officer absently scored one point too many. Silvio took the chalk and noted down the correct account according to his usual custom. The officer, thinking that he had made a mistake, began to enter into explanations. Silvio continued dealing in silence. The officer, losing patience, took the brush and rubbed out what he considered was wrong. Silvio took the chalk and corrected the score again. The officer, heated with wine, play, and the laughter of his comrades, considered himself grossly insulted, and in his rage he seized a brass candlestick from the table, and hurled it at Silvio, who barely succeeded in avoiding the missile. We were filled with consternation. Silvio rose, white with rage, and with gleaming eyes, said:

"My dear sir, have the goodness to withdraw, and thank God that this has happened in my house."

None of us entertained the slightest doubt as to what the result would be, and we already looked upon our new comrade as a dead man. The officer withdrew, saying that he was ready to answer for his offence in whatever way the banker liked. The play went on for a few minutes longer, but feeling that our host was no longer interested in the game, we withdrew one after the other, and repaired to our respective quarters, after having exchanged a few words upon the probability of there soon being a vacancy in the regiment.

The next day, at the riding-school, we were already asking each other if the poor lieutenant was still alive, when he himself appeared among us. We put the same question to him, and he replied that he had not yet heard from Silvio. This astonished us. We went to Silvio's house and found him in the courtyard shooting bullet after bullet into an ace pasted upon the gate. He received us as usual, but did not utter a word about the event of the previous evening. Three days passed, and the lieutenant was still alive. We asked each other in astonishment: "Can it be possible that Silvio is not going to fight?"

Silvio did not fight. He was satisfied with a very lame explanation, and became reconciled to his assailant.

This lowered him very much in the opinion of all our young fellows. Want of courage is the last thing to be pardoned by young men, who usually look upon bravery as the chief of all human virtues, and the excuse for every possible fault. But, by degrees, everything became forgotten, and Silvio regained his former influence.

I alone could not approach him on the old footing. Being endowed by nature with a romantic imagination, I had become attached more than all the others to the man whose life was an enigma, and who seemed to me the hero of some mysterious drama. He was fond of me; at least, with me alone did he drop his customary sarcastic tone, and converse on different subjects in a simple and unusually agreeable manner. But after this unlucky evening, the thought that his honour had been tarnished, and that the stain had been allowed to remain upon it in accordance with his own wish, was ever present in my mind, and prevented me treating him as before. I was ashamed to look at him. Silvio was too intelligent and experienced not to observe this and guess the cause of it. This seemed to vex him; at least I observed once or twice a desire on his part to enter into an explanation with me, but I avoided such opportunities, and Silvio gave up the attempt. From that time forward I saw him only in the presence of my comrades, and our confidential conversations came to an end.

The inhabitants of the capital, with minds occupied by so many matters of business and pleasure, have no idea of the many sensations so familiar to the inhabitants of villages and small towns, as, for instance, the awaiting the arrival of the post. On Tuesdays and Fridays our regimental bureau used to be filled with officers: some expecting money, some letters, and others newspapers. The packets were usually opened on the spot, items of news were communicated from one to another, and the bureau used to present a very animated picture. Silvio used to have his letters addressed to our regiment, and he was generally there to receive them.

One day he received a letter, the seal of which he broke with a look of great impatience. As he read the contents, his eyes sparkled. The officers, each occupied with his own letters, did not observe anything.

"Gentlemen," said Silvio, "circumstances demand my immediate departure; I leave to-night. I hope that you will not refuse to dine with me for the last time. I shall expect you, too," he added, turning towards me. "I shall expect you without fail."

With these words he hastily departed, and we, after agreeing to meet at Silvio's, dispersed to our various quarters.

I arrived at Silvio's house at the appointed time, and found nearly the whole regiment there. All his things were already packed; nothing remained but the bare, bullet-riddled walls. We sat down to table. Our host was in an excellent humour, and his gaiety was quickly communicated to the rest. Corks popped every moment, glasses foamed incessantly, and, with the utmost warmth, we wished our departing friend a pleasant journey and every happiness. When we rose from the table it was already late in the evening. After having wished everybody good-bye, Silvio took me by the hand and detained me just at the moment when I was preparing to depart.

"I want to speak to you," he said in a low voice.

I stopped behind.

The guests had departed, and we two were left alone. Sitting down opposite each other, we silently lit our pipes. Silvio seemed greatly troubled; not a trace remained of his former convulsive gaiety. The intense pallor of his face, his sparkling eyes, and the thick smoke issuing from his mouth, gave him a truly diabolical appearance. Several minutes elapsed, and then Silvio broke the silence.

"Perhaps we shall never see each other again," said he; "before we part, I should like to have an explanation with you. You may have observed that I care very little for the opinion of other people, but I like you, and I feel that it would be painful to me to leave you with a wrong impression upon your mind."

He paused, and began to knock the ashes out of his pipe. I sat gazing silently at the ground.

"You thought it strange," he continued, "that I did not demand satisfaction from that drunken idiot R——. You will admit, however, that having the choice of weapons, his life was in my hands, while my own was in no great danger. I could ascribe my forbearance to generosity alone, but I will not tell a lie. If I could have chastised R—— without the least risk to my own life, I should never have pardoned him."

I looked at Silvio with astonishment. Such a confession completely astounded me. Silvio continued:

"Exactly so: I have no right to expose myself to death. Six years ago I received a slap in the face, and my enemy still lives."

My curiosity was greatly excited.

"Did you not fight with him?" I asked. "Circumstances probably separated you."

"I did fight with him," replied Silvio: "and here is a souvenir of our duel."

Silvio rose and took from a cardboard box a red cap with a gold tassel and embroidery (what the French call a *bonnet de police*); he put it on ——a bullet had passed through it about an inch above the forehead.

"You know," continued Silvio, "that I served in one of the Hussar regiments. My character is well-known to you: I am accustomed to taking the lead. From my youth this has been my passion. In our time dissoluteness was the fashion, and I was the most outrageous man in the army. We used to boast of our drunkenness: I beat in a drinking bout the famous Bourtsoff,[1] of whom Denis Davidoff[2] has sung. Duels in our regiment were constantly taking place, and in all of them I was either second or principal. My comrades adored me, while the regimental commanders, who were constantly being changed, looked upon me as a necessary evil.

"I was calmly enjoying my reputation, when a young man belonging to a wealthy and distinguished family — I will not mention his name — joined our regiment. Never in my life have I met with such a fortunate fellow! Imagine to yourself youth, wit, beauty, unbounded gaiety, the most reckless bravery, a famous name, untold wealth — imagine all these, and you can form some idea of the effect that he would be sure to produce among us. My supremacy was shaken. Dazzled by my reputation, he began to seek my friendship, but I received him coldly, and without the least regret he held aloof from me. I took a hatred to him. His success in the regiment and in the society of ladies brought me to the verge of despair. I began to seek a quarrel with him; to my epigrams he replied with epigrams which always seemed to me more spontaneous and more cutting than mine, and which were decidedly more amusing, for he joked while I fumed. At last, at a ball given by a Polish landed proprietor, seeing him the object of the attention of all the ladies, and especially of the mistress of the house, with whom I was upon very good terms, I whispered some grossly insulting remark in his ear. He flamed up and gave me a slap in the face. We grasped our swords; the ladies fainted; we were separated; and that same night we set out to fight.

[1] A cavalry officer, notorious for his drunken escapades.
[2] A military poet who flourished in the reign of Alexander I.

"The dawn was just breaking. I was standing at the appointed place with my three seconds. With inexplicable impatience I awaited my opponent. The spring sun rose, and it was already growing hot. I saw him coming in the distance. He was walking on foot, accompanied by one second. We advanced to meet him. He approached, holding his cap filled with black cherries. The seconds measured twelve paces for us. I had to fire first, but my agitation was so great, that I could not depend upon the steadiness of my hand; and in order to give myself time to become calm, I ceded to him the first shot. My adversary would not agree to this. It was decided that we should cast lots. The first number fell to him, the constant favourite of fortune. He took aim, and his bullet went through my cap. It was now my turn. His life at last was in my hands; I looked at him eagerly, endeavouring to detect if only the faintest shadow of uneasiness. But he stood in front of my pistol, picking out the ripest cherries from his cap and spitting out the stones, which flew almost as far as my feet. His indifference annoyed me beyond measure. 'What is the use,' thought I, 'of depriving him of life, when he attaches no value whatever to it?' A malicious thought flashed through my mind. I lowered my pistol.

" 'You don't seem to be ready for death just at present,' I said to him: 'you wish to have your breakfast; I do not wish to hinder you.'

" 'You are not hindering me in the least,' replied he. 'Have the goodness to fire, or just as you please — the shot remains yours; I shall always be ready at your service.'

"I turned to the seconds, informing them that I had no intention of firing that day, and with that the duel came to an end.

"I resigned my commission and retired to this little place. Since then, not a day has passed that I have not thought of revenge. And now my hour has arrived."

Silvio took from his pocket the letter that he had received that morning, and gave it to me to read. Someone (it seemed to be his business agent) wrote to him from Moscow, that a *certain person* was going to be married to a young and beautiful girl.

"You can guess," said Silvio, "who the certain person is. I am going to Moscow. We shall see if he will look death in the face with as much indifference now, when he is on the eve of being married, as he did once with his cherries!"

With these words, Silvio rose, threw his cap upon the floor, and began pacing up and down the room like a tiger in his cage. I had listened to him in silence; strange conflicting feelings agitated me.

The servant entered and announced that the horses were ready. Silvio grasped my hand tightly, and we embraced each other. He seated himself in his *telega*, in which lay two trunks, one containing his pistols, the other his effects. We said good-bye once more, and the horses galloped off.

CHAPTER II.

SEVERAL YEARS PASSED, and family circumstances compelled me to settle in the poor little village of M——. Occupied with agricultural pursuits, I ceased not to sigh in secret for my former noisy and careless life. The most difficult thing of all was having to accustom myself to passing the spring and winter evenings in perfect solitude. Until the hour for dinner I managed to pass away the time somehow or other, talking with the bailiff, riding about to inspect the work, or going round to look at the new buildings; but as soon as it began to get dark, I positively did not know what to do with myself. The few books that I had found in the cupboards and store-rooms, I already knew by heart. All the stories that my housekeeper Kirilovna could remember, I had heard over and over again. The songs of the peasant woman made me feel depressed. I tried drinking spirits, but it made my head ache; and moreover, I confess I was afraid of becoming a drunkard from mere chagrin, that is to say, the saddest kind of drunkard, of which I had seen many examples in our district.

I had no near neighbours, except two or three topers, whose conversation consisted for the most part of hiccups and sighs. Solitude was preferable to their society. At last I decided to go to bed as early as possible, and to dine as late as possible; in this way I shortened the evening and lengthened out the day, and I found that the plan answered very well.

Four versts from my house was a rich estate belonging to the Countess B——; but nobody lived there except the steward. The Countess had only visited her estate once, in the first year of her married life, and then she had remained there no longer than a month. But in the second spring of my hermitical life, a report was circulated that the Countess, with her husband, was coming to spend the summer on her estate. The report turned out to be true, for they arrived at the beginning of June.

The arrival of a rich neighbour is an important event in the lives of country people. The landed proprietors and the people of their household talk about it for two months beforehand, and for three years afterward. As for me, I must confess that the news of the arrival of a young and beautiful neighbour affected me strongly. I burned with impatience to see her, and the first Sunday after her arrival I set out after dinner for the village of A——, to pay my respects to the Countess and her husband, as their nearest neighbour and most humble servant.

A lackey conducted me into the Count's study, and then went to announce me. The spacious apartment was furnished with every possible luxury. Around the walls were cases filled with books and surmounted by bronze busts; over the marble mantelpiece was a large mirror; on the floor was a green cloth covered with carpets. Unaccustomed to luxury in my own poor corner, and not having seen the wealth of other people for a long time, I awaited the appearance of the Count with some little trepidation, as a suppliant from the provinces awaits the arrival of the minister. The door opened, and a handsome-looking man, of about thirty-two years of age, entered the room. The Count approached me with a frank and friendly air: I endeavoured to be self-possessed and began to introduce myself, but he anticipated me. We sat down. His conversation, which was easy and agreeable, soon dissipated my awkward bashfulness; and I was already beginning to recover my usual composure, when the Countess suddenly entered, and I became more confused than ever. She was indeed beautiful. The Count presented me. I wished to appear at ease, but the more I tried to assume an air of unconstraint, the more awkward I felt. They, in order to give me time to recover myself and to become accustomed to my new acquaintances, began to talk to each other, treating me as a good neighbour, and without ceremony. Meanwhile, I walked about the room, examining the books and pictures. I am no judge of pictures, but one of them attracted my attention. It represented some view in Switzerland, but it was not the painting that struck me, but the circumstance that the canvas was shot through by two bullets, one planted just above the other.

"A good shot, that!" said I, turning to the Count.

"Yes," replied he, "a very remarkable shot. . . . Do you shoot well?" he continued.

"Tolerably," replied I, rejoicing that the conversation had turned at last upon a subject that was familiar to me. "At thirty paces I can manage to hit a card without fail, — I mean, of course, with a pistol that I am used to."

"Really?" said the Countess, with a look of the greatest interest. "And you, my dear, could you hit a card at thirty paces?"

"Some day," replied the Count, "we will try. In my time I did not shoot badly, but it is now four years since I touched a pistol."

"Oh!" I observed, "in that case, I don't mind laying a wager that Your Excellency will not hit the card at twenty paces: the pistol demands practice every day. I know that from experience. In our regiment I was reckoned one of the best shots. It once happened that I did not touch a pistol for a whole month, as I had sent mine to be mended; and would you believe it, Your Excellency, the first time I began to shoot again, I missed a bottle four times in succession at twenty paces! Our captain, a witty and amusing fellow, happened to be standing by, and he said to me: 'It is evident, my friend, that your hand will not lift itself against the bottle.' No, Your Excellency, you must not neglect to practise, or your hand will soon lose its cunning. The best shot that I ever met used to shoot at least three times every day before dinner. It was as much his custom to do this, as it was to drink his daily glass of brandy."

The Count and Countess seemed pleased that I had begun to talk.

"And what sort of a shot was he?" asked the Count.

"Well, it was this way with him, Your Excellency: if he saw a fly settle on the wall — you smile, Countess, but, before Heaven, it is the truth. If he saw a fly, he would call out: 'Kouzka, my pistol!' Kouzka would bring him a loaded pistol — bang! and the fly would be crushed against the wall."

"Wonderful!" said the Count. "And what was his name?"

"Silvio, Your Excellency."

"Silvio!" exclaimed the Count, starting up. "Did you know Silvio?"

"How could I help knowing him, Your Excellency: we were intimate friends; he was received in our regiment like a brother officer, but it is now five years since I had any tidings of him. Then Your Excellency also knew him?"

"Oh, yes, I knew him very well. Did he ever tell you of one very strange incident in his life?"

"Does Your Excellency refer to the slap in the face that he received from some blackguard at a ball?"

"Did he ever tell you the name of this blackguard?"

"No, Your Excellency, he never mentioned his name. . . . Ah! Your Excellency!" I continued, guessing the truth: "pardon me . . . I did not know . . . could it really have been you?"

"Yes, I myself," replied the Count, with a look of extraordinary agitation; "and that bullet-pierced picture is a memento of our last meeting."

"Ah, my dear," said the Countess, "for Heaven's sake, do not speak about that; it would be too terrible for me to listen to."

"No," replied the Count: "I will relate everything. He knows how I insulted his friend, and it is only right that he should know how Silvio revenged himself."

The Count pushed a chair towards me, and with the liveliest interest I listened to the following story:

"Five years ago I got married. The first month — the honeymoon — I spent here, in this village. To this house I am indebted for the happiest moments of my life, as well as for one of its most painful recollections.

"One evening we went out together for a ride on horseback. My wife's horse became restive; she grew frightened, gave the reins to me, and returned home on foot. I rode on before. In the courtyard I saw a travelling carriage, and I was told that in my study sat waiting for me a man, who would not give his name, but who merely said that he had business with me. I entered the room and saw in the darkness a man, covered with dust and wearing a beard of several days' growth. He was standing there, near the fireplace. I approached him, trying to remember his features.

" 'You do not recognize me, Count?' said he, in a quivering voice.

" 'Silvio!' I cried, and I confess that I felt as if my hair had suddenly stood on end.

" 'Exactly,' continued he. 'There is a shot due to me, and I have come to discharge my pistol. Are you ready?'

"His pistol protruded from a side pocket. I measured twelve paces and took my stand there in that corner, begging him to fire quickly, before my wife arrived. He hesitated, and asked for a light. Candles were brought in. I closed the doors, gave orders that nobody was to enter, and again begged him to fire. He drew out his pistol and took aim. . . . I counted the seconds . . . I thought of her . . . A terrible minute passed! Silvio lowered his hand.

" 'I regret,' said he, 'that the pistol is not loaded with cherry-stones . . . the bullet is heavy. It seems to me that this is not a duel, but a murder. I am not accustomed to taking aim at unarmed men. Let us begin all over again; we will cast lots as to who shall fire first.'

"My head went round . . . I think I raised some objection. . . . At last we loaded another pistol, and rolled up two pieces of paper. He placed these latter in his cap — the same through which I had once sent a bullet — and again I drew the first number.

" 'You are devilish lucky, Count,' said he, with a smile that I shall never forget.

"I don't know what was the matter with me, or how it was that he managed to make me do it . . . but I fired and hit that picture."

The Count pointed with his finger to the perforated picture; his face glowed like fire; the Countess was whiter than her own handkerchief; and I could not restrain an exclamation.

"I fired," continued the Count, "and, thank Heaven, missed my aim. Then Silvio . . . at that moment he was really terrible. . . . Silvio raised his hand to take aim at me. Suddenly the door opens, Masha rushes into the room, and with a loud shriek throws herself upon my neck. Her presence restored to me all my courage.

" 'My dear,' said I to her, 'don't you see that we are joking? How frightened you are! Go and drink a glass of water and then come back to us; I will introduce you to an old friend and comrade.'

"Masha still doubted.

" 'Tell me, is my husband speaking the truth?' said she, turning to the terrible Silvio: 'is it true that you are only joking?'

" 'He is always joking, Countess,' replied Silvio: 'once he gave me a slap in the face in a joke; on another occasion he sent a bullet through my cap in a joke; and just now, when he fired at me and missed me, it was all in a joke. And now I feel inclined for a joke.'

"With these words he raised his pistol to take aim at me — right before her! Masha threw herself at his feet.

" 'Rise, Masha; are you not ashamed!' I cried in a rage: 'and you, sir, will you cease to make fun of a poor woman? Will you fire or not?'

" 'I will not,' replied Silvio: 'I am satisfied. I have seen your confusion, your alarm. I forced you to fire at me. That is sufficient. You will remember me. I leave you to your conscience.'

"Then he turned to go, but pausing in the doorway, and looking at the picture that my shot had passed through, he fired at it almost without taking aim, and disappeared. My wife had fainted away; the servants did not venture to stop him, the mere look of him filled them with terror. He went out upon the steps, called his coachman, and drove off before I could recover myself."

The Count was silent. In this way I learned the end of the story, whose beginning had once made such a deep impression upon me. The hero of it I never saw again. It is said that Silvio commanded a detachment of Hetairists during the revolt under Alexander Ipsilanti, and that he was killed in the battle of Skoulana.*

* [A battle waged by one group of Greek freedom fighters, the Hetairists, against Turkish domination.]

The Snowstorm.

TOWARDS THE END of the year 1811, a memorable period for us, the good Gavril Gavrilovitch R—— was living on his domain of Nenaradova. He was celebrated throughout the district for his hospitality and kindheartedness. The neighbours were constantly visiting him: some to eat and drink; some to play at five copeck "Boston" with his wife, Praskovia Petrovna; and some to look at their daughter, Maria Gavrilovna, a pale, slender girl of seventeen. She was considered a wealthy match, and many desired her for themselves or for their sons.

Maria Gavrilovna had been brought up on French novels, and consequently was in love. The object of her choice was a poor sub-lieutenant in the army, who was then on leave of absence in his village. It need scarcely be mentioned that the young man returned her passion with equal ardour, and that the parents of his beloved one, observing their mutual inclination, forbade their daughter to think of him, and received him worse than a discharged assessor.

Our lovers corresponded with one another and daily saw each other alone in the little pine wood or near the old chapel. There they exchanged vows of eternal love, lamented their cruel fate, and formed various plans. Corresponding and conversing in this way, they arrived quite naturally at the following conclusion:

If we cannot exist without each other, and the will of hard-hearted parents stands in the way of our happiness, why cannot we do without them?

Needless to mention that this happy idea originated in the mind of the young man, and that it was very congenial to the romantic imagination of Maria Gavrilovna.

The winter came and put a stop to their meetings, but their correspondence became all the more active. Vladimir Nikolaievitch in every letter implored her to give herself up to him, to get married secretly, to hide for some time, and then throw themselves at the feet of their parents, who would, without any doubt, be touched at last by the heroic constancy and unhappiness of the lovers, and would infallibly say to them: "Children, come to our arms!"

Maria Gavrilovna hesitated for a long time, and several plans for a flight were rejected. At last she consented: on the appointed day she was not to take supper, but was to retire to her room under the pretext of a headache. Her maid was in the plot; they were both to go into the garden by the back stairs, and behind the garden they would find ready a sledge, into which they were to get, and then drive straight to the church of Jadrino, a village about five versts from Nenaradova, where Vladimir would be waiting for them.

On the eve of the decisive day, Maria Gavrilovna did not sleep the whole night; she packed and tied up her linen and other articles of apparel, wrote a long letter to a sentimental young lady, a friend of hers, and another to her parents. She took leave of them in the most touching terms, urged the invincible strength of passion as an excuse for the step she was taking, and wound up with the assurance that she should consider it the happiest moment of her life, when she should be allowed to throw herself at the feet of her dear parents.

After having sealed both letters with a Toula seal, upon which were engraved two flaming hearts with a suitable inscription, she threw herself upon her bed just before daybreak, and dozed off: but even then she was constantly being awakened by terrible dreams. First it seemed to her that at the very moment when she seated herself in the sledge, in order to go and get married, her father stopped her, dragged her over the snow with fearful rapidity, and threw her into a dark bottomless abyss, down which she fell headlong with an indescribable sinking of the heart. Then she saw Vladimir lying on the grass, pale and bloodstained. With his dying breath he implored her in a piercing voice to make haste and marry him. . . . Other fantastic and senseless visions floated before her one after another. At last she arose, paler than usual, and with an unfeigned headache. Her father and mother observed her uneasiness; their tender solicitude and incessant inquiries: "What is the matter with you, Masha? Are you ill, Masha?" cut her to the heart. She tried to reassure them and to appear cheerful, but in vain.

The evening came. The thought, that this was the last day she would pass in the bosom of her family, weighed upon her heart. She was more dead than alive. In secret she took leave of everybody, of all the objects that surrounded her.

Supper was served; her heart began to beat violently. In a trembling voice she declared that she did not want any supper, and then took leave of her father and mother. They kissed her and blessed her as usual, and she could hardly restrain herself from weeping.

On reaching her own room, she threw herself into a chair and burst into tears. Her maid urged her to be calm and to take courage. Everything was ready. In half an hour Masha would leave for ever her parents' house, her room, and her peaceful girlish life. . . .

Out in the courtyard the snow was falling heavily; the wind howled, the shutters shook and rattled, and everything seemed to her to portend misfortune.

Soon all was quiet in the house: everyone was asleep. Masha wrapped herself in a shawl, put on a warm cloak, took her small box in her hand, and went down the back staircase. Her maid followed her with two bundles. They descended into the garden. The snowstorm had not subsided; the wind blew in their faces, as if trying to stop the young criminal. With difficulty they reached the end of the garden. In the road a sledge awaited them. The horses, half-frozen with the cold, would not keep still; Vladimir's coachman was walking up and down in front of them, trying to restrain their impatience. He helped the young lady and her maid into the sledge, placed the box and the bundles in the vehicle, seized the reins, and the horses dashed off.

Having intrusted the young lady to the care of fate and to the skill of Tereshka the coachman, we will return to our young lover.

Vladimir had spent the whole of the day in driving about. In the morning he paid a visit to the priest of Jadrino, and having come to an agreement with him after a great deal of difficulty, he then set out to seek for witnesses among the neighbouring landowners. The first to whom he presented himself, a retired cornet* of about forty years of age, and whose name was Dravin, consented with pleasure. The adventure, he declared, reminded him of his young days and his pranks in the Hussars. He persuaded Vladimir to stay to dinner with him, and assured him that he would have no difficulty in finding the other two witnesses. And, indeed, immediately after dinner, appeared the surveyor Schmidt, with moustache and spurs, and the son of the captain of police, a lad of sixteen years of age, who had recently entered the Uhlans. They not only accepted Vladimir's proposal, but even vowed that they were ready to sacrifice their lives for him. Vladimir embraced them with rapture, and returned home to get everything ready.

It had been dark for some time. He dispatched his faithful Tereshka to Nenaradova with his sledge and with detailed instructions, and ordered for himself the small sledge with one horse, and set out alone, without any coachman, for Jadrino, where Maria Gavrilovna ought to arrive in about a couple of hours. He knew the road well, and the journey would only occupy about twenty minutes altogether.

* [Lowest rank of cavalry officer.]

But scarcely had Vladimir issued from the paddock into the open field, when the wind rose and such a snowstorm came on that he could see nothing. In one minute the road was completely hidden; all surrounding objects disappeared in a thick yellow fog, through which fell the white flakes of snow; earth and sky became confounded. Vladimir found himself in the middle of the field, and tried in vain to find the road again. His horse went on at random, and at every moment kept either stepping into a snowdrift or stumbling into a hole, so that the sledge was constantly being overturned. Vladimir endeavoured not to lose the right direction. But it seemed to him that more than half an hour had already passed, and he had not yet reached the Jadrino wood. Another ten minutes elapsed — still no wood was to be seen. Vladimir drove across a field intersected by deep ditches. The snowstorm did not abate, the sky did not become any clearer. The horse began to grow tired, and the perspiration rolled from him in great drops, in spite of the fact that he was constantly being half-buried in the snow.

At last Vladimir perceived that he was going in the wrong direction. He stopped, began to think, to recollect, and compare, and he felt convinced that he ought to have turned to the right. He turned to the right now. His horse could scarcely move forward. He had now been on the road for more than an hour. Jadrino could not be far off. But on and on he went, and still no end to the field — nothing but snowdrifts and ditches. The sledge was constantly being overturned, and as constantly being set right again. The time was passing: Vladimir began to grow seriously uneasy.

At last something dark appeared in the distance. Vladimir directed his course towards it. On drawing near, he perceived that it was a wood.

"Thank Heaven!" he thought, "I am not far off now."

He drove along by the edge of the wood, hoping by-and-by to fall upon the well-known road or to pass round the wood: Jadrino was situated just behind it. He soon found the road, and plunged into the darkness of the wood, now denuded of leaves by the winter. The wind could not rage here; the road was smooth; the horse recovered courage, and Vladimir felt reassured.

But he drove on and on, and Jadrino was not to be seen; there was no end to the wood. Vladimir discovered with horror that he had entered an unknown forest. Despair took possession of him. He whipped the horse; the poor animal broke into a trot, but it soon slackened its pace, and in about a quarter of an hour it was scarcely able to drag one leg after the other, in spite of all the exertions of the unfortunate Vladimir.

Gradually the trees began to get sparser, and Vladimir emerged from the forest; but Jadrino was not to be seen. It must now have been about midnight. Tears gushed from his eyes; he drove on at random. Meanwhile the storm had subsided, the clouds dispersed, and before him lay a level plain covered with a white undulating carpet. The night was tolerably clear. He saw, not far off, a little village, consisting of four or five houses. Vladimir drove towards it. At the first cottage he jumped out of the sledge, ran to the window and began to knock. After a few minutes, the wooden shutter was raised, and an old man thrust out his grey beard.

"What do you want?"

"Is Jadrino far from here?"

"Is Jadrino far from here?"

"Yes, yes! Is it far?"

"Not far; about ten versts."

At this reply, Vladimir grasped his hair and stood motionless, like a man condemned to death.

"Where do you come from?" continued the old man.

Vladimir had not the courage to answer the question.

"Listen, old man," said he: "can you procure me horses to take me to Jadrino?"

"How should we have such things as horses?" replied the peasant.

"Can I obtain a guide? I will pay him whatever he pleases."

"Wait," said the old man, closing the shutter; "I will send my son out to you; he will guide you."

Vladimir waited. But a minute had scarcely elapsed when he began knocking again. The shutter was raised, and the beard again appeared.

"What do you want?"

"What about your son?"

"He'll be out presently; he is putting on his boots. Are you cold? Come in and warm yourself."

"Thank you; send your son out quickly."

The door creaked: a lad came out with a cudgel and went on in front, at one time pointing out the road, at another searching for it among the drifted snow.

"What is the time?" Vladimir asked him.

"It will soon be daylight," replied the young peasant. Vladimir spoke not another word.

The cocks were crowing, and it was already light when they reached Jadrino. The church was closed. Vladimir paid the guide and drove into the priest's courtyard. His sledge was not there. What news awaited him! . . . . . .

But let us return to the worthy proprietors of Nenaradova, and see what is happening there.

Nothing.

The old people awoke and went into the parlour, Gavril Gavrilovitch in a night-cap and flannel doublet, Praskovia Petrovna in a wadded dressing-gown. The tea-urn was brought in, and Gavril Gavrilovitch sent a servant to ask Maria Gavrilovna how she was and how she had passed the night. The servant returned, saying that the young lady had not slept very well, but that she felt better now, and that she would come down presently into the parlour. And indeed, the door opened and Maria Gavrilovna entered the room and wished her father and mother good morning.

"How is your head, Masha?" asked Gavril Gavrilovitch.

"Better, papa," replied Masha.

"Very likely you inhaled the fumes from the charcoal yesterday," said Praskovia Petrovna.

"Very likely, mamma," replied Masha.

The day passed happily enough, but in the night Masha was taken ill. A doctor was sent for from the town. He arrived in the evening and found the sick girl delirious. A violent fever ensued, and for two weeks the poor patient hovered on the brink of the grave.

Nobody in the house knew anything about her flight. The letters, written by her the evening before, had been burnt; and her maid, dreading the wrath of her master, had not whispered a word about it to anybody. The priest, the retired cornet, the moustached surveyor, and the little Uhlan were discreet, and not without reason. Tereshka, the coachman, never uttered one word too much about it, even when he was drunk. Thus the secret was kept by more than half-a-dozen conspirators.

But Maria Gavrilovna herself divulged her secret during her delirious ravings. But her words were so disconnected, that her mother, who never left her bedside, could only understand from them that her daughter was deeply in love with Vladimir Nikolaievitch, and that probably love was the cause of her illness. She consulted her husband and some of her neighbours, and at last it was unanimously decided that such was evidently Maria Gavrilovna's fate, that a woman cannot ride away from the man who is destined to be her husband, that poverty is not a crime, that one does not marry wealth, but a man, etc., etc. Moral proverbs are wonderfully useful in those cases where we can invent little in our own justification.

In the meantime the young lady began to recover. Vladimir had not been seen for a long time in the house of Gavril Gavrilovitch. He was afraid of the usual reception. It was resolved to send and announce to him an unexpected piece of good news: the consent of Maria's parents to his marriage with their daughter. But what was the astonishment of the proprietor of Nenaradova, when, in reply to their invitation, they received from him a half-insane letter. He informed them that he would never set foot in their house again, and begged them to forget an unhappy creature whose only hope was in death. A few days afterwards they heard that Vladimir had joined the army again. This was in the year 1812.

For a long time they did not dare to announce this to Masha, who was now convalescent. She never mentioned the name of Vladimir. Some months afterwards, finding his name in the list of those who had distinguished themselves and been severely wounded at Borodino,[1] she fainted away, and it was feared that she would have another attack of fever. But, Heaven be thanked! the fainting fit had no serious consequences.

Another misfortune fell upon her: Gavril Gavrilovitch died, leaving her the heiress to all his property. But the inheritance did not console her; she shared sincerely the grief of poor Praskovia Petrovna, vowing that she would never leave her. They both quitted Nenaradova, the scene of so many sad recollections, and went to live on another estate.

Suitors crowded round the young and wealthy heiress, but she gave not the slightest hope to any of them. Her mother sometimes exhorted her to make a choice; but Maria Gavrilovna shook her head and became pensive. Vladimir no longer existed: he had died in Moscow on the eve of the entry of the French. His memory seemed to be held sacred by Masha; at least she treasured up everything that could remind her of him: books that he had once read, his drawings, his notes, and verses of poetry that he had copied out for her. The neighbours, hearing of all this, were astonished at her constancy, and awaited with curiosity the hero who should at last triumph over the melancholy fidelity of this virgin Artemisia.*

Meanwhile the war had ended gloriously. Our regiments returned from abroad, and the people went out to meet them. The bands played the conquering songs: "Vive Henri-Quatre," Tyrolese waltzes and airs

[1] A village about fifty miles from Moscow, and the scene of a sanguinary battle between the French and Russian forces during the invasion of Russia by Napoleon I.

* [Wife of Mausolus, 4th century B.C. emperor of Caria; she had the original Mausoleum built in memory of her husband.]

from "Joconde." Officers, who had set out for the war almost mere lads, returned grown men, with martial air, and their breasts decorated with crosses. The soldiers chatted gaily among themselves, constantly mingling French and German words in their speech. Time never to be forgotten! Time of glory and enthusiasm! How throbbed the Russian heart at the word "Fatherland!" How sweet were the tears of meeting! With what unanimity did we unite feelings of national pride with love for the Czar! And for him — what a moment!

The women, the Russian women, were then incomparable. Their usual coldness disappeared. Their enthusiasm was truly intoxicating, when welcoming the conquerors they cried "Hurrah!"

"And threw their caps high in the air!"[1]

What officer of that time does not confess that to the Russian women he was indebted for his best and most precious reward?

At this brilliant period Maria Gavrilovna was living with her mother in the province of ——, and did not see how both capitals celebrated the return of the troops. But in the districts and villages the general enthusiasm was, if possible, even still greater. The appearance of an officer in those places was for him a veritable triumph, and the lover in a plain coat felt very ill at ease in his vicinity.

We have already said that, in spite of her coldness, Maria Gavrilovna was, as before, surrounded by suitors. But all had to retire into the background when the wounded Colonel Bourmin of the Hussars, with the Order of St. George in his button-hole, and with an "interesting pallor," as the young ladies of the neighbourhood observed, appeared at the castle. He was about twenty-six years of age. He had obtained leave of absence to visit his estate, which was contiguous to that of Maria Gavrilovna. Maria bestowed special attention upon him. In his presence her habitual pensiveness disappeared. It cannot be said that she coquetted with him, but a poet, observing her behaviour, would have said:

"Se amor non è, che dunque?"[2]

Bourmin was indeed a very charming young man. He possessed that spirit which is eminently pleasing to women: a spirit of decorum and observation, without any pretensions, and yet not without a slight tendency towards careless satire. His behaviour towards Maria Gavrilovna was simple and frank, but whatever she said or did, his soul and eyes

---

[1] Griboiedoff.
[2] ["If it isn't love, then what is it?" (Petrarch).]

followed her. He seemed to be of a quiet and modest disposition, though report said that he had once been a terrible rake; but this did not injure him in the opinion of Maria Gavrilovna, who — like all young ladies in general — excused with pleasure follies that gave indication of boldness and ardour of temperament.

But more than everything else — more than his tenderness, more than his agreeable conversation, more than his interesting pallor, more than his arm in a sling, — the silence of the young Hussar excited her curiosity and imagination. She could not but confess that he pleased her very much; probably he, too, with his perception and experience, had already observed that she made a distinction between him and others; how was it then that she had not yet seen him at her feet or heard his declaration? What restrained him? Was it timidity, inseparable from true love, or pride, or the coquetry of a crafty wooer? It was an enigma to her. After long reflection, she came to the conclusion that timidity alone was the cause of it, and she resolved to encourage him by greater attention and, if circumstances should render it necessary, even by an exhibition of tenderness. She prepared a most unexpected dénouement, and waited with impatience for the moment of the romantic explanation. A secret, of whatever nature it may be, always presses heavily upon the female heart. Her stratagem had the desired success; at least Bourmin fell into such a reverie, and his black eyes rested with such fire upon her, that the decisive moment seemed close at hand. The neighbours spoke about the marriage as if it were a matter already decided upon, and good Praskovia Petrovna rejoiced that her daughter had at last found a lover worthy of her.

On one occasion the old lady was sitting alone in the parlour, amusing herself with a pack of cards, when Bourmin entered the room and immediately inquired for Maria Gavrilovna.

"She is in the garden," replied the old lady: "go out to her, and I will wait here for you."

Bourmin went, and the old lady made the sign of the cross and thought: "Perhaps the business will be settled to-day!"

Bourmin found Maria Gavrilovna near the pond, under a willow-tree, with a book in her hands, and in a white dress: a veritable heroine of romance. After the first few questions and observations, Maria Gavrilovna purposely allowed the conversation to drop, thereby increasing their mutual embarrassment, from which there was no possible way of escape except only by a sudden and decisive declaration.

And this is what happened: Bourmin, feeling the difficulty of his position, declared that he had long sought for an opportunity to open his heart to her, and requested a moment's attention. Maria Gavrilovna closed her book and cast down her eyes, as a sign of compliance with his request.

"I love you," said Bourmin: "I love you passionately. . . ."

Maria Gavrilovna blushed and lowered her head still more. "I have acted imprudently in accustoming myself to the sweet pleasure of seeing and hearing you daily. . . ." Maria Gavrilovna recalled to mind the first letter of St. Preux.[1] "But it is now too late to resist my fate; the remembrance of you, your dear incomparable image, will henceforth be the torment and the consolation of my life, but there still remains a grave duty for me to perform—to reveal to you a terrible secret which will place between us an insurmountable barrier. . . ."

"That barrier has always existed," interrupted Maria Gavrilovna hastily: "I could never be your wife."

"I know," replied he calmly: "I know that you once loved, but death and three years of mourning. . . . Dear, kind Maria Gavrilovna, do not try to deprive me of my last consolation: the thought that you would have consented to make me happy, if——"

"Don't speak, for Heaven's sake, don't speak. You torture me."

"Yes, I know, I feel that you would have been mine, but—I am the most miserable creature under the sun—I am already married!"

Maria Gavrilovna looked at him in astonishment.

"I am already married," continued Bourmin: "I have been married four years, and I do not know who is my wife, or where she is, or whether I shall ever see her again!"

"What do you say?" exclaimed Maria Gavrilovna. "How very strange! Continue: I will relate to you afterwards. . . . But continue, I beg of you."

"At the beginning of the year 1812," said Bourmin, "I was hastening to Vilna, where my regiment was stationed. Arriving late one evening at one of the post-stations, I ordered the horses to be got ready as quickly as possible, when suddenly a terrible snowstorm came on, and the postmaster and drivers advised me to wait till it had passed over. I followed their advice, but an unaccountable uneasiness took possession of me: it seemed as if someone were pushing me forward. Meanwhile the snowstorm did not subside; I could endure it no longer, and again ordering out the horses, I started off in the midst of the storm. The driver conceived the idea of following the course of the river, which would shorten our journey by three versts. The banks were covered with snow:

---

[1] In "La Nouvelle Héloïse," by Jean-Jacques Rousseau.

the driver drove past the place where we should have come out upon the road, and so we found ourselves in an unknown part of the country. . . . The storm did not cease; I saw a light in the distance, and I ordered the driver to proceed towards it. We reached a village; in the wooden church there was a light. The church was open. Outside the railings stood several sledges, and people were passing in and out through the porch.

" 'This way! this way!' cried several voices.

"I ordered the driver to proceed.

" 'In the name of Heaven, where have you been loitering?' said somebody to me. 'The bride has fainted away; the pope does not know what to do, and we were just getting ready to go back. Get out as quickly as you can.'

"I got out of the sledge without saying a word, and went into the church, which was feebly lit up by two or three tapers. A young girl was sitting on a bench in a dark corner of the church; another girl was rubbing her temples.

" 'Thank God!' said the latter, 'you have come at last. You have almost killed the young lady.'

"The old priest advanced towards me, and said:

" 'Do you wish me to begin?'

" 'Begin, begin, father,' replied I, absently.

"The young girl was raised up. She seemed to me not at all bad-looking. . . . Impelled by an incomprehensible, unpardonable levity, I placed myself by her side in front of the pulpit; the priest hurried on; three men and a chambermaid supported the bride and only occupied themselves with her. We were married.

" 'Kiss each other!' said the witnesses to us.

"My wife turned her pale face towards me. I was about to kiss her, when she exclaimed: 'Oh! it is not he! it is not he!' and fell senseless.

"The witnesses gazed at me in alarm. I turned round and left the church without the least hindrance, flung myself into the *kibitka* and cried: 'Drive off!'

"My God!" exclaimed Maria Gavrilovna. "And you do not know what became of your poor wife?"

"I do not know," replied Bourmin; "neither do I know the name of the village where I was married, nor the post-station where I set out from. At that time I attached so little importance to my wicked prank, that on leaving the church, I fell asleep, and did not awake till the next morning after reaching the third station. The servant, who was then with me, died during the campaign, so that I have no hope of ever discovering the woman upon whom I played such a cruel joke, and who is now so cruelly avenged."

"My God! my God!" cried Maria Gavrilovna, seizing him by the hand: "then it was you! And you do not recognize me?"

Bourmin turned pale — and threw himself at her feet.

The Postmaster.

This tyrant, a collegiate recorder,
Still keeps the posting station in good order.

Prince Vyazemsky

WHO HAS NOT cursed postmasters, who has not quarreled with them? Who, in a moment of anger, has not demanded from them the fatal book in order to record in it unavailing complaints of their extortions, rudeness and carelessness? Who does not look upon them as monsters of the human race, equal to the attorneys of old, or, at least, the Murom highwaymen? Let us, however, be just; let us place ourselves in their position, and perhaps we shall begin to judge them with more indulgence. What is a postmaster? A veritable martyr of the fourteenth class,[1] protected by his rank from blows only, and that not always (I appeal to the conscience of my readers). What is the function of this tyrant, as Prince Vyazemsky jokingly calls him? Is he not an actual galley-slave? He has no rest either day or night. All the vexation accumulated during the course of a wearisome journey the traveller vents upon the postmaster. Should the weather prove intolerable, the road abominable, the driver obstinate, the horses stubborn — the postmaster is to blame. Entering into his poor abode, the traveller looks upon him as an enemy, and the postmaster is fortunate if he succeeds in soon getting rid of his unbidden guest; but if there should happen to be no horses! ... Heavens! what volleys of abuse, what threats are showered upon his head! When it rains, when it is muddy, he is compelled to run about the village; during times of storm and bitter frost, he is glad to seek shelter in the entry, if only to enjoy a minute's repose from the shouting and jostling of incensed travellers.

A general arrives: the trembling postmaster gives him the two last *troikas*, including that intended for the courier. The general drives off without uttering a word of thanks. Five minutes afterwards — a bell! ... and a courier throws down upon the table before him his order for fresh post-horses! ... Let us bear all this well in mind, and, instead of anger, our hearts will be filled with sincere compassion. A few words more. During a period of twenty years I have traversed Russia in every direction; I know nearly all the post roads, and I am acquainted with several generations of drivers. There are very few postmasters that I do not know

---

[1] The officials of Russia were divided into fourteen classes, the fourteenth being the lowest.

personally, and few with whom I have not had something to do. I hope shortly to publish the curious observations that I have noted down during my travels. For the present I will only say that the class of postmasters is presented to the public in a very false light. These much-calumniated officials are generally very peaceful persons, obliging by nature, disposed to be sociable, modest in their pretensions to honours and not too greedy. From their conversation (which travelling gentlemen very unreasonably scorn) much may be learnt that is both curious and instructive. For my own part, I confess that I prefer their talk to that of some official of the sixth class travelling on government business.

It may easily be supposed that I have friends among the honourable body of postmasters. Indeed, the memory of one of them is precious to me. Circumstances once brought us together, and it is of him that I now intend to tell my amiable readers.

In the month of May of the year 1816, I happened to be travelling through the X. Government, along a route that has since been abandoned. I then held an inferior rank, and I travelled by post stages, paying the fare for two horses. As a consequence, the postmasters treated me with very little ceremony, and I often had to take by force what, in my opinion, belonged to me by right. Being young and hot-tempered, I was indignant at the baseness and cowardice of the postmaster, when the latter harnessed to the coach of some gentleman of rank, the horses prepared for me. It was a long time, too, before I could get accustomed to being served out of my turn by a discriminating flunkey at the governor's dinner. Today the one and the other seem to me to be in the natural order of things. Indeed, what would become of us, if, instead of the generally observed rule: "Let rank honour rank," another were to be brought into use, as for example: "Let mind honour mind?" What disputes would arise! And whom would the butler serve first? But to return to my story.

The day was hot. About three versts from the N. station a drizzling rain came on, and in a few minutes it began to pour down in torrents and I was drenched to the skin. On arriving at the station, my first care was to change my clothes as quickly as possible, my second to ask for some tea.

"Hi! Dunya!"[1] cried the postmaster: "prepare the samovar and go and get some cream."

At these words, a young girl of about fourteen years of age appeared from behind the partition, and ran out into the entry. Her beauty struck me.

[1] Diminutive of Avdotya.

"Is that your daughter?" I inquired of the postmaster.

"That is my daughter," he replied, with a look of gratified pride; "and she is so sharp and sensible, just like her late mother."

Then he began to register my travelling passport, and I occupied myself with examining the pictures that adorned his humble but tidy abode. They illustrated the story of the Prodigal Son. In the first, a venerable old man, in a night-cap and dressing-gown, was taking leave of the restless lad, who was hastily accepting his blessing and a bag of money. In the next picture, the dissolute conduct of the young man was depicted in vivid colors: he was represented sitting at table surrounded by false friends and shameless women. Further on, the ruined youth, in rags and a three-cornered hat, was tending swine and sharing with them their food: his face expressed deep grief and repentance. The last picture represented his return to his father: the good old man, in the same night-cap and dressing-gown, runs forward to meet him; the prodigal son is on his knees; in the distance the cook is killing the fatted calf, and the elder brother is asking the servants the cause of all the rejoicing. Under each picture I read some suitable German verses. All this I have preserved in my memory to the present day, as well as the little pots of balsamine, the bed with gay curtains, and the other objects with which I was then surrounded. I can see, as though he were before me, the host himself, a man of about fifty years of age, healthy and vigorous, in his long green coat with three medals on faded ribbons.

I had scarcely settled my account with my old driver, when Dunya returned with the samovar. The little coquette saw at the second glance the impression she had produced upon me; she lowered her large blue eyes; I began to talk to her; she answered me without the least timidity, like a girl who has seen the world. I offered her father a glass of punch, to Dunya herself I gave a cup of tea, and then the three of us began to converse together, as if we were old acquaintances.

The horses had long been ready, but I felt reluctant to take leave of the postmaster and his daughter. At last I bade them good-bye, the father wished me a pleasant journey, the daughter accompanied me to the coach. In the entry I stopped and asked her permission to kiss her; Dunya consented. . . . I can reckon up a great many kisses

Since first I chose this occupation,

but not one which has left behind such a long, such a pleasant recollection.

Several years passed, and circumstances led me to the same route, and to the same neighbourhood.

"But," thought I, "perhaps the old postmaster has been changed, and Dunya may already be married."

The thought that one or the other of them might be dead also flashed through my mind, and I approached the N. station with a sad foreboding. The horses drew up before the little post-house. On entering the room, I immediately recognized the pictures illustrating the story of the Prodigal Son. The table and the bed stood in the same places as before, but the flowers were no longer on the window-sills, and everything around indicated decay and neglect.

The postmaster was asleep under his sheep-skin coat; my arrival awoke him, and he stood up. . . . It was certainly Samson Vyrin, but how aged! While he was preparing to register my travelling passport, I gazed at his gray hair, the deep wrinkles upon his face, that had not been shaved for a long time, his bent back, and I was astonished to see how three or four years had been able to transform a vigorous individual into a feeble old man.

"Do you recognize me?" I asked him: "we are old acquaintances."

"Maybe," replied he sullenly; "this is a high road, and many travellers have stopped here."

"Is your Dunya well?" I continued.

The old man frowned.

"God knows," he replied.

"Probably she is married?" said I.

The old man pretended not to have heard my question, and went on reading my passport in a low tone. I ceased questioning him and ordered some tea. Curiosity began to torment me, and I hoped that the punch would loosen the tongue of my old acquaintance.

I was not mistaken; the old man did not refuse the proffered glass. I observed that the rum dispelled his sullenness. At the second glass he began to talk; he remembered me, or appeared to do so, and I heard from him a story, which at the time, deeply interested and affected me.

"So you knew my Dunya?" he began. "But who did not know her? Ah, Dunya, Dunya! What a girl she was! Everybody who passed this way praised her; nobody had a word to say against her. The ladies used to give her presents — now a handkerchief, now a pair of earrings. The gentlemen used to stop on purpose, as if to dine or to take supper, but in reality only to take a longer look at her. However angry a gentleman might be, in her presence he grew calm and spoke graciously to me. Would you believe it, sir: couriers and government messengers used to talk to her for half an hour at a stretch. It was she held the home together; she put everything in order, got everything ready, and looked after everything.

And I, like an old fool, could not look at her enough, could not idolize her enough. Did I not love my Dunya? Did I not indulge my child? Was not her life a happy one? But no, there is no escaping misfortune: there is no evading what has been decreed."

Then he began to tell me the story of his trouble in detail. Three years earlier, one winter evening, when the postmaster was ruling a new register, and his daughter behind the partition was sewing a dress, a *troika* drove up, and a traveller in a Circassian cap and military cloak, and enveloped in a shawl, entered the room and demanded horses. The horses were all out. On being told this, the traveller raised his voice and whip; but Dunya, accustomed to such scenes, ran out from behind the partition and graciously inquired of the traveller whether he would not like something to eat and drink.

The appearance of Dunya produced the usual effect. The traveller's anger subsided; he consented to wait for horses, and ordered supper. Having taken off his wet shaggy cap, and divested himself of his shawl and cloak, the traveller was seen to be a tall, young Hussar with a small black mustache. He settled down, and began to converse gaily with the postmaster and his daughter. Supper was served. Meanwhile the horses returned, and the postmaster ordered them, without being fed, to be harnessed immediately to the traveller's *kibitka*. But on returning to the room, he found the young man lying almost unconscious on the bench; he had been taken ill, his head ached, it was impossible for him to continue his journey. What was to be done? The postmaster gave up his own bed to him, and it was decided that if the sick man did not get better, they would send next day to S—— for the doctor.

The next day the Hussar was worse. His servant rode to town for a doctor. Dunya bound round his head a handkerchief soaked in vinegar, and sat with her needlework beside his bed. In the presence of the postmaster, the sick man groaned and scarcely uttered a word; but he drank two cups of coffee, and, groaning, ordered dinner. Dunya did not quit his side. He constantly asked for something to drink, and Dunya gave him a jug of lemonade prepared by herself. The sick man moistened his lips, and each time, on returning the jug, he feebly pressed Dunya's hand in token of gratitude.

About dinner time the doctor arrived. He felt the sick man's pulse, spoke to him in German, and declared in Russian that he only needed rest, and that in about a couple of days he would be able to set out on his journey. The Hussar gave him twenty-five rubles for his visit, and invited him to dinner; the doctor consented. They both ate with great appetite, drank a bottle of wine, and separated very well satisfied with each other.

Another day passed, and the Hussar felt quite himself again. He was extraordinarily gay, joked unceasingly, now with Dunya, now with the postmaster, whistled tunes, chatted with the travellers, copied their passports into the register, and the worthy postmaster took such a fancy to him that when the third day arrived, it was with regret that he parted with his amiable guest.

The day was Sunday; Dunya was preparing to go to mass. The Hussar's *kibitka* stood ready. He took leave of the postmaster, after having generously recompensed him for his board and lodging, bade farewell to Dunya, and offered to drive her as far as the church, which was situated at the edge of the village. Dunya hesitated.

"What are you afraid of?" asked her father. "His Excellency is not a wolf: he won't eat you. Drive with him as far as the church."

Dunya seated herself in the *kibitka* by the side of the Hussar, the servant sprang upon the box, the driver whistled, and the horses started off at a gallop.

The poor postmaster could not understand how he could have allowed his Dunya to drive off with the Hussar, how he could have been so blind, and what had become of his senses at that moment. A half-hour had not elapsed, before his heart began to ache, and uneasiness took possession of him to such a degree, that he could contain himself no longer, and started off for mass himself. On reaching the church, he saw that the people were already beginning to disperse, but Dunya was neither in the churchyard nor in the porch. He hastened into the church: the priest was leaving the chancel, the sexton was blowing out the candles, two old women were still praying in a corner, but Dunya was not in the church. The poor father was scarcely able to summon up sufficient resolution to ask the sexton if she had been to mass. The sexton replied that she had not. The postmaster returned home neither alive nor dead. One hope alone remained to him: Dunya, in the thoughtlessness of youth, might have taken it into her head to go on as far as the next station, where her godmother lived. In agonizing agitation he awaited the return of the *troika* in which he had let her set out. There was no sign of it. At last, in the evening, the driver arrived alone and intoxicated, with the terrible news: "Dunya went on with the Hussar from the next station."

The old man could not bear his misfortune: he immediately took to that very same bed where, the evening before, the young deceiver had lain. Taking all the circumstances into account, the postmaster now came to the conclusion that the illness had been a mere pretence. The poor man fell ill with a violent fever; he was removed to S——, and in his place another person was appointed for the time being. The same doctor, who had attended the Hussar, attended him also. He assured the postmaster that the young man had been perfectly well, and that at the time of his visit he had suspected him of some evil intention, but that he had kept silent through fear of his whip. Whether the German spoke the truth or only wished to boast of his perspicacity, his communication afforded no consolation to the poor invalid. Scarcely had the latter recovered from his illness, when he obtained from the postmaster of S—— two months' leave of absence, and without saying a word to anybody of his intention, he set out on foot in search of his daughter.

From the travelling passport he knew that Captain Minsky was journeying from Smolensk to St. Petersburg. The driver with whom he had gone off said that Dunya had wept the whole of the way, although she seemed to go of her own free will.

"Perhaps," thought the postmaster, "I shall bring my lost lamb home again."

With this thought he reached St. Petersburg, stopped in the neighbourhood of the Izmailovsky barracks, at the house of a retired corporal, an old comrade of his, and began his search. He soon discovered that Captain Minsky was in St. Petersburg, and was living at Demoute's Inn. The postmaster resolved to call upon him.

Early in the morning he went to Minsky's ante-chamber, and requested that His Excellency might be informed that an old soldier wished to see him. The orderly, who was just then polishing a boot on a boot-tree, informed him that his master was still asleep, and that he never received anybody before eleven o'clock. The postmaster retired and returned at the appointed time. Minsky himself came out to him in his dressing-gown and red skull-cap.

"Well, brother, what do you want?" he asked.

The old man's heart was wrung, tears started to his eyes, and he was only able to say in a trembling voice:

"Your Excellency! . . . do me the great favour! . . ."

Minsky glanced quickly at him, flushed, took him by the hand, led him into his study and locked the door.

"Your Excellency!" continued the old man: "what has fallen from the load is lost; give me back at least my poor Dunya. You have had your pleasure with her; do not ruin her for nothing."

"What is done cannot be undone," said the young man, in the utmost confusion; "I am guilty before you, and am ready to ask your pardon, but do not think that I could forsake Dunya: she will be happy, I give you my word of honour. Why do you want her? She loves me; she has become unaccustomed to her former way of living. Neither you nor she will forget what has happened."

Then, pushing something into the old man's cuff, he opened the door, and the postmaster, without remembering how, found himself in the street again.

For a long time he stood motionless; at last he observed in the cuff of his sleeve a roll of papers; he drew them out and unrolled several fifty-ruble notes. Tears again filled his eyes, tears of indignation! He crushed the notes into a ball, flung them upon the ground, stamped upon them with the heel of his boot, and then walked away. . . . After having gone a few steps, he stopped, reflected, and returned . . . but the notes were no longer there. A well-dressed young man, noticing him, ran toward a *droshky*, jumped in hurriedly, and cried to the driver: "Go on!"

The postmaster did not pursue him. He resolved to return home to his station, but before doing so he wished to see his poor Dunya once more. For that purpose, he returned to Minsky's lodgings a couple of days later, but when he came the orderly told him roughly that his master received nobody, pushed him out of the ante-chamber and slammed the door in his face. The postmaster stood waiting for a long time, then he walked away.

That same day, in the evening, he was walking along Liteinaia Street, having been to a service at the Church of Our Lady of All the Sorrowing. Suddenly a smart *droshky* flew past him, and the postmaster recognized Minsky. The *droshky* stopped in front of a three-story house, close to the entrance, and the Hussar ran up the steps. A happy thought flashed through the mind of the postmaster. He returned, and, approaching the coachman:

"Whose horse is this, my friend?" asked he: "Doesn't it belong to Minsky?"

"Exactly so," replied the coachman: "what do you want?"

"Well, your master ordered me to carry a letter to his Dunya, and I have forgotten where his Dunya lives."

"She lives here, on the second floor. But you are late with your letter, my friend; he is with her himself just now."

"That doesn't matter," replied the postmaster, with an indescribable emotion. "Thanks for your information. I shall do as I was told." And with these words he ascended the staircase.

The door was locked; he rang. There was a painful delay of several seconds. The key rattled, and the door was opened.

"Does Avdotya Samsonovna live here?" he asked.

"Yes," replied a young maidservant: "what do you want with her?"

The postmaster, without replying, walked into the room.

"You mustn't go in, you mustn't go in!" the servant cried out after him: "Avdotya Samsonovna has visitors."

But the postmaster, without heeding her, walked straight on. The first two rooms were dark; in the third there was a light. He approached the open door and paused. In the room, which was beautifully furnished, sat Minsky in deep thought. Dunya, attired in the most elegant fashion, was sitting upon the arm of his chair, like a lady rider upon her English saddle. She was gazing tenderly at Minsky, and winding his black curls round her dazzling fingers. Poor postmaster! Never had his daughter seemed to him so beautiful; he admired her against his will.

"Who is there?" she asked, without raising her head.

He remained silent. Receiving no reply, Dunya raised her head . . . and with a cry she fell upon the carpet. The alarmed Minsky hastened to pick her up, but suddenly catching sight of the old postmaster in the doorway, he left Dunya and approached him, trembling with rage.

"What do you want?" he said to him, clenching his teeth. "Why do you steal after me everywhere, like a thief? Or do you want to murder me? Be off!" and with a powerful hand he seized the old man by the collar and pushed him out onto the stairs.

The old man returned to his lodgings. His friend advised him to lodge a complaint, but the postmaster reflected, waved his hand, and resolved to abstain from taking any further steps in the matter. Two days afterward he left St. Petersburg and returned to his station to resume his duties.

"This is the third year," he concluded, "that I have been living without Dunya, and I have not heard a word about her. Whether she is alive or not—God only knows. So many things happen. She is not the first, nor yet the last, that a travelling scoundrel has seduced, kept for a little while, and then abandoned. There are many such young fools in St. Petersburg, today in satin and velvet, and tomorrow sweeping the streets along with the riff-raff of the dram-shops. Sometimes, when I think that Dunya also may come to such an end, then, in spite of myself, I sin and wish her in her grave. . . ."

Such was the story of my friend, the old postmaster, a story more than once interrupted by tears, which he picturesquely wiped away with the skirt of his coat, like the zealous Terentyich in Dmitriyev's beautiful ballad.* These tears were partly induced by the punch, of which he had drunk five glasses during the course of his narrative, but for all that, they

* [A comic ballad, "The Retired Sergeant Major."]

moved me deeply. After taking leave of him, it was a long time before I could forget the old postmaster, and for a long time I thought of poor Dunya. . . .

Passing through the little town of X. a short time ago, I remembered my friend. I heard that the station, over which he ruled, had been done away with. To my question: "Is the old postmaster still alive?" nobody could give me a satisfactory reply. I resolved to pay a visit to the familiar place, and having hired horses, I set out for the village of N——.

It was in the autumn. Gray clouds covered the sky; a cold wind blew across the reaped fields, carrying along with it the red and yellow leaves from the trees that it encountered. I arrived in the village at sunset, and stopped at the little post-house. In the entry (where Dunya had once kissed me) a stout woman came out to meet me, and in answer to my questions replied, that the old postmaster had been dead for about a year, that his house was occupied by a brewer, and that she was the brewer's wife. I began to regret my useless journey, and the seven rubles that I had spent in vain.

"Of what did he die?" I asked the brewer's wife.

"Of drink, sir," she replied.

"And where is he buried?"

"On the outskirts of the village, near his late wife."

"Could somebody take me to his grave?"

"To be sure! Hi, Vanka, you have played with that cat long enough. Take this gentleman to the cemetery, and show him the postmaster's grave."

At these words a ragged lad, with red hair, and blind in one eye, ran up to me and immediately began to lead the way toward the burial-ground.

"Did you know the dead man?" I asked him on the road.

"Yes, indeed! He taught me how to cut whistles. When he came out of the dram-shop (God rest his soul!) we used to run after him and call out: 'Grandfather! grandfather! some nuts!' and he used to throw nuts to us. He always used to play with us."

"And do the travellers remember him?"

"There are very few travellers now; the assessor passes this way some-times, but he doesn't trouble himself about dead people. Last summer a lady passed through here, and she asked after the old postmaster, and went to his grave."

"What sort of a lady?" I asked with curiosity.

"A very beautiful lady," replied the lad. "She was in a carriage with six horses, and had along with her three little children, a nurse, and a little black lapdog; and when they told her that the old postmaster was dead, she began to cry, and said to the children: 'Sit still, I will go to the cemetery.' I offered to show her the way. But the lady said: 'I know the way.' And she gave me a five-copeck piece. . . . such a kind lady!"

We reached the cemetery, a bare place, with no fence around it, dotted with wooden crosses, which were not shaded by a single tree. Never in my life had I seen such a dismal cemetery.

"This is the old postmaster's grave," said the lad to me, leaping upon a heap of sand, in which was planted a black cross with a bronze ikon.

"And did the lady come here?" I asked.

"Yes," replied Vanka; "I watched her from a distance. She cast herself down here, and remained lying down for a long time. Then she went back to the village, sent for the priest, gave him some money and drove off, after giving me a five-copeck piece. . . . such a kind lady!"

And I, too, gave the lad a five-copeck piece, and I no longer regretted the journey nor the seven rubles that I had spent on it.

The Coffin-Maker.

THE LAST OF the effects of the coffin-maker, Adrian Prokhoroff, were placed upon the hearse, and a couple of sorry-looking jades dragged themselves along for the fourth time from Basmannaia to Nikitskaia,* whither the coffin-maker was removing with all his household. After locking up the shop, he posted upon the door a placard announcing that the house was to be let or sold, and then made his way on foot to his new abode. On approaching the little yellow house, which had so long captivated his imagination, and which at last he had bought for a considerable sum, the old coffin-maker was astonished to find that his heart did not rejoice. When he crossed the unfamiliar threshold and found his new home in the greatest confusion, he sighed for his old hovel, where for eighteen years the strictest order had prevailed. He began to scold his two daughters and the servant for their slowness, and then set to work to help them himself. Order was soon established; the ark with the sacred images, the cupboard with the crockery, the table, the sofa, and the bed occupied the corners reserved for them in the back room; in the kitchen and parlour were placed the articles comprising the stock-in-trade of the master—coffins of all colours and of all sizes, together with cupboards containing mourning hats, cloaks and torches.

Over the door was placed a sign representing a fat Cupid with an inverted torch in his hand and bearing this inscription: "Plain and coloured coffins sold and lined here; coffins also let out on hire, and old ones repaired."

The girls retired to their bedroom; Adrian made a tour of inspection of his quarters, and then sat down by the window and ordered the tea-urn to be prepared.

The enlightened reader knows that Shakespeare and Walter Scott have both represented their grave-diggers as merry and facetious individuals, in order that the contrast might more forcibly strike our imagination. Out of respect for the truth, we cannot follow their example, and we are compelled to confess that the disposition of our coffin-maker was in perfect harmony with his gloomy occupation. Adrian Prokhoroff was usually gloomy and thoughtful. He rarely opened his mouth, except to scold his daughters when he found them standing idle and gazing out of

* [Streets in Moscow.]

the window at the passers by, or to demand for his wares an exorbitant price from those who had the misfortune — and sometimes the good fortune — to need them. Hence it was that Adrian, sitting near the window and drinking his seventh cup of tea, was immersed as usual in melancholy reflections. He thought of the pouring rain which, just a week before, had commenced to beat down during the funeral of the retired brigadier. Many of the cloaks had shrunk in consequence of the downpour, and many of the hats had been put quite out of shape. He foresaw unavoidable expenses, for his old stock of funeral dresses was in a pitiable condition. He hoped to compensate himself for his losses by the burial of old Trukhina, the shopkeeper's wife, who for more than a year had been upon the point of death. But Trukhina lay dying at Rasgouliai,* and Prokhoroff was afraid that her heirs, in spite of their promise, would not take the trouble to send so far for him, but would make arrangements with the nearest undertaker.

These reflections were suddenly interrupted by three masonic knocks at the door.

"Who is there?" asked the coffin-maker.

The door opened, and a man, who at the first glance could be recognized as a German artisan, entered the room, and with a jovial air advanced towards the coffin-maker.

"Pardon me, respected neighbour," said he in that Russian dialect which to this day we cannot hear without a smile: "pardon me for disturbing you. . . . I wished to make your acquaintance as soon as possible. I am a shoemaker, my name is Gottlieb Schultz, and I live across the street, in that little house just facing your windows. To-morrow I am going to celebrate my silver wedding, and I have come to invite you and your daughters to dine with us."

The invitation was cordially accepted. The coffin-maker asked the shoemaker to seat himself and take a cup of tea, and thanks to the open-hearted disposition of Gottlieb Schultz, they were soon engaged in friendly conversation.

"How is business with you?" asked Adrian.

"Just so so," replied Schultz; "I cannot complain. My wares are not like yours: the living can do without shoes, but the dead cannot do without coffins."

"Very true," observed Adrian; "but if a living person hasn't anything to buy shoes with, you cannot find fault with him, he goes about bare-footed; but a dead beggar gets his coffin for nothing."

* [Locality in Moscow.]

In this manner the conversation was carried on between them for some time; at last the shoemaker rose and took leave of the coffin-maker, renewing his invitation.

The next day, exactly at twelve o'clock, the coffin-maker and his daughters issued from the doorway of their newly-purchased residence, and directed their steps towards the abode of their neighbour. I will not stop to describe the Russian *caftan* of Adrian Prokhoroff, nor the European toilettes of Akoulina and Daria, deviating in this respect from the usual custom of modern novelists. But I do not think it superfluous to observe that they both had on the yellow cloaks and red shoes, which they were accustomed to don on solemn occasions only.

The shoemaker's little dwelling was filled with guests, consisting chiefly of German artisans with their wives and foremen. Of the Russian officials there was present but one, Yourko the Finn, a watchman, who, in spite of his humble calling, was the special object of the host's attention. For twenty-five years he had faithfully discharged the duties of postilion of Pogorelsky. The conflagration of 1812, which destroyed the ancient capital, destroyed also his little yellow watch-house. But immediately after the expulsion of the enemy, a new one appeared in its place, painted grey and with white Doric columns, and Yourko began again to pace to and fro before it, with his axe and grey coat of mail. He was known to the greater part of the Germans who lived near the Nikitskaia Gate, and some of them had even spent the night from Sunday to Monday beneath his roof.

Adrian immediately made himself acquainted with him, as with a man whom, sooner or later, he might have need of, and when the guests took their places at the table, they sat down beside each other. Herr Schultz and his wife, and their daughter Lotchen, a young girl of seventeen, did the honours of the table and helped the cook to serve. The beer flowed in streams; Yourko ate like four, and Adrian in no way yielded to him; his daughters, however, stood upon their dignity. The conversation, which was carried on in German, gradually grew more and more boisterous. Suddenly the host requested a moment's attention, and uncorking a sealed bottle, he said with a loud voice in Russian:

"To the health of my good Louise!"

The champagne foamed. The host tenderly kissed the fresh face of his partner, and the guests drank noisily to the health of the good Louise.

"To the health of my amiable guests!" exclaimed the host, uncorking a second bottle; and the guests thanked him by draining their glasses once more.

Then followed a succession of toasts. The health of each individual guest was drunk; they drank to the health of Moscow and to quite a dozen little German towns; they drank to the health of all corporations in general and of each in particular; they drank to the health of the masters and foremen. Adrian drank with enthusiasm and became so merry, that he proposed a facetious toast to himself. Suddenly one of the guests, a fat baker, raised his glass and exclaimed:

"To the health of those for whom we work, our customers!"

This proposal, like all the others, was joyously and unanimously received. The guests began to salute each other; the tailor bowed to the shoemaker, the shoemaker to the tailor, the baker to both, the whole company to the baker, and so on. In the midst of these mutual congratulations, Yourko exclaimed, turning to his neighbour:

"Come, little father! Drink to the health of your corpses!"

Everybody laughed, but the coffin-maker considered himself insulted, and frowned. Nobody noticed it, the guests continued to drink, and the bell had already rung for vespers when they rose from the table.

The guests dispersed at a late hour, the greater part of them in a very merry mood. The fat baker and the bookbinder, whose face seemed as if bound in red morocco, linked their arms in those of Yourko and conducted him back to his little watch-house, thus observing the proverb: "One good turn deserves another."

The coffin-maker returned home drunk and angry.

"Why is it," he exclaimed aloud, "why is it that my trade is not as honest as any other? Is a coffin-maker brother to the hangman? Why did those heathens laugh? Is a coffin-maker a buffoon? I wanted to invite them to my new dwelling and give them a feast, but now I'll do nothing of the kind. Instead of inviting them, I will invite those for whom I work: the orthodox dead."

"What is the matter, little father?" said the servant, who was engaged at that moment in taking off his boots: "why do you talk such nonsense? Make the sign of the cross! Invite the dead to your new house! What folly!"

"Yes, by the Lord! I will invite them," continued Adrian, "and that, too, for to-morrow! . . . Do me the favour, my benefactors, to come and feast with me to-morrow evening; I will regale you with what God has sent me."

With these words the coffin-maker turned into bed and soon began to snore.

It was still dark when Adrian was awakened out of his sleep. Trukhina, the shopkeeper's wife, had died during the course of that very night, and a special messenger was sent off on horseback by her bailiff to carry the news to Adrian. The coffin-maker gave him ten copecks to buy brandy with, dressed himself as hastily as possible, took a *droshky* and set out for Rasgouliai. Before the door of the house in which the deceased lay, the police had already taken their stand, and the trades-people were passing backwards and forwards, like ravens that smell a dead body. The deceased lay upon a table, yellow as wax, but not yet disfigured by decomposition. Around her stood her relatives, neighbours and domestic servants. All the windows were open; tapers were burning; and the priests were reading the prayers for the dead. Adrian went up to the nephew of Trukhina, a young shopman in a fashionable surtout, and informed him that the coffin, wax candles, pall, and the other funeral accessories would be immediately delivered with all possible exactitude. The heir thanked him in an absent-minded manner, saying that he would not bargain about the price, but would rely upon him acting in everything according to his conscience. The coffin-maker, in accordance with his usual custom, vowed that he would not charge him too much, exchanged significant glances with the bailiff, and then departed to commence operations.

The whole day was spent in passing to and fro between Rasgouliai and the Nikitskaia Gate. Towards evening everything was finished, and he returned home on foot, after having dismissed his driver. It was a moonlight night. The coffin-maker reached the Nikitskaia Gate in safety. Near the Church of the Ascension he was hailed by our acquaintance Yourko, who, recognizing the coffin-maker, wished him good-night. It was late. The coffin-maker was just approaching his house, when suddenly he fancied he saw some one approach his gate, open the wicket, and disappear within.

"What does that mean?" thought Adrian. "Who can be wanting me again? Can it be a thief come to rob me? Or have my foolish girls got lovers coming after them? It means no good, I fear!"

And the coffin-maker thought of calling his friend Yourko to his assistance. But at that moment, another person approached the wicket and was about to enter, but seeing the master of the house hastening towards him, he stopped and took off his three-cornered hat. His face seemed familiar to Adrian, but in his hurry he had not been able to examine it closely.

"You are favouring me with a visit," said Adrian, out of breath. "Walk in, I beg of you."

"Don't stand on ceremony, little father," replied the other, in a hollow voice; "you go first, and show your guests the way."

Adrian had no time to spend upon ceremony. The wicket was open; he ascended the steps followed by the other. Adrian thought he could hear people walking about in his rooms.

"What the devil does all this mean!" he thought to himself, and he hastened to enter. But the sight that met his eyes caused his legs to give way beneath him.

The room was full of corpses. The moon, shining through the windows, lit up their yellow and blue faces, sunken mouths, dim, half-closed eyes, and protruding noses. Adrian, with horror, recognized in them people that he himself had buried, and in the guest who entered with him, the brigadier who had been buried during the pouring rain. They all, men and women, surrounded the coffin-maker, with bowings and salutations, except one poor fellow lately buried gratis, who, conscious and ashamed of his rags, did not venture to approach, but meekly kept aloof in a corner. All the others were decently dressed: the female corpses in caps and ribbons, the officials in uniforms, but with their beards unshaven, the tradesmen in their holiday *caftans*.

"You see, Prokhoroff," said the brigadier in the name of all the honourable company, "we have all risen in response to your invitation. Only those have stopped at home who were unable to come, who have crumbled to pieces and have nothing left but fleshless bones. But even of these there was one who hadn't the patience to remain behind — so much did he want to come and see you. . . ."

At this moment a little skeleton pushed his way through the crowd and approached Adrian. His fleshless face smiled affably at the coffin-maker. Shreds of green and red cloth and rotten linen hung on him here and there as on a pole, and the bones of his feet rattled inside his big jack-boots, like pestles in mortars.

"You do not recognize me, Prokhoroff," said the skeleton. "Don't you remember the retired sergeant of the Guards, Peter Petrovitch Kourilkin, the same to whom, in the year 1799, you sold your first coffin, and that, too, of deal instead of oak?"

With these words the corpse stretched out his bony arms towards him; but Adrian, collecting all his strength, shrieked and pushed him from him. Peter Petrovitch staggered, fell, and crumbled all to pieces. Among the corpses arose a murmur of indignation; all stood up for the honour of their companion, and they overwhelmed Adrian with such threats and imprecations, that the poor host, deafened by their shrieks and almost crushed to death, lost his presence of mind, fell upon the bones of the retired sergeant of the Guards, and swooned away.

For some time the sun had been shining upon the bed on which lay the coffin-maker. At last he opened his eyes and saw before him the servant attending to the tea-urn. With horror, Adrian recalled all the incidents of the previous day. Trukhina, the brigadier, and the sergeant, Kourilkin, rose vaguely before his imagination. He waited in silence for the servant to open the conversation and inform him of the events of the night.

"How you have slept, little father Adrian Prokhorovitch!" said Aksinia, handing him his dressing-gown. "Your neighbour, the tailor, has been here, and the watchman also called to inform you that to-day is his name-day; but you were so sound asleep, that we did not wish to wake you."

"Did anyone come for me from the late Trukhina?"

"The late? Is she dead, then?"

"What a fool you are! Didn't you yourself help me yesterday to prepare the things for her funeral?"

"Have you taken leave of your senses, little father, or have you not yet recovered from the effects of yesterday's drinking-bout? What funeral was there yesterday? You spent the whole day feasting at the German's, and then came home drunk and threw yourself upon the bed, and have slept till this hour, when the bells have already rung for mass."

"Really!" said the coffin-maker, greatly relieved.

"Yes, indeed," replied the servant.

"Well, since that is the case, make the tea as quickly as possible and call my daughters."

DOVER · THRIFT · EDITIONS

POETRY

GUNGA DIN AND OTHER FAVORITE POEMS, Rudyard Kipling. 80pp. 26471-8

SNAKE AND OTHER POEMS, D. H. Lawrence. 64pp. 40647-4

THE CONGO AND OTHER POEMS, Vachel Lindsay. 96pp. 27272-9

EVANGELINE AND OTHER POEMS, Henry Wadsworth Longfellow. 64pp. 28255-4

FAVORITE POEMS, Henry Wadsworth Longfellow. 96pp. 27273-7

"TO HIS COY MISTRESS" AND OTHER POEMS, Andrew Marvell. 64pp. 29544-3

SPOON RIVER ANTHOLOGY, Edgar Lee Masters. 144pp. 27275-3

SELECTED POEMS, Claude McKay. 80pp. 40876-0

RENASCENCE AND OTHER POEMS, Edna St. Vincent Millay. 64pp. (Available in U.S. only.) 26873-X

SELECTED POEMS, John Milton. 128pp. 27554-X

CIVIL WAR POETRY: An Anthology, Paul Negri (ed.). 128pp. 29883-3

ENGLISH VICTORIAN POETRY: AN ANTHOLOGY, Paul Negri (ed.). 256pp. 40425-0

GREAT SONNETS, Paul Negri (ed.). 96pp. 28052-7

THE RAVEN AND OTHER FAVORITE POEMS, Edgar Allan Poe. 64pp. 26685-0

ESSAY ON MAN AND OTHER POEMS, Alexander Pope. 128pp. 28053-5

EARLY POEMS, Ezra Pound. 80pp. (Available in U.S. only.) 28745-9

GREAT POEMS BY AMERICAN WOMEN: An Anthology, Susan L. Rattiner (ed.). 224pp. (Available in U.S. only.) 40164-2

LITTLE ORPHANT ANNIE AND OTHER POEMS, James Whitcomb Riley. 80pp. 28260-0

GOBLIN MARKET AND OTHER POEMS, Christina Rossetti. 64pp. 28055-1

CHICAGO POEMS, Carl Sandburg. 80pp. 28057-8

CORNHUSKERS, Carl Sandburg. 157pp. 41409-4

THE SHOOTING OF DAN MCGREW AND OTHER POEMS, Robert Service. 96pp. (Available in U.S. only.) 27556-6

COMPLETE SONNETS, William Shakespeare. 80pp. 26686-9

SELECTED POEMS, Percy Bysshe Shelley. 128pp. 27558-2

AFRICAN-AMERICAN POETRY: An Anthology, 1773–1930, Joan R. Sherman (ed.). 96pp. 29604-0

100 BEST-LOVED POEMS, Philip Smith (ed.). 96pp. 28553-7

NATIVE AMERICAN SONGS AND POEMS: An Anthology, Brian Swann (ed.). 64pp. 29450-1

SELECTED POEMS, Alfred Lord Tennyson. 112pp. 27282-6

AENEID, Vergil (Publius Vergilius Maro). 256pp. 28749-1

CHRISTMAS CAROLS: COMPLETE VERSES, Shane Weller (ed.). 64pp. 27397-0

GREAT LOVE POEMS, Shane Weller (ed.). 128pp. 27284-2

CIVIL WAR POETRY AND PROSE, Walt Whitman. 96pp. 28507-3

SELECTED POEMS, Walt Whitman. 128pp. 26878-0

THE BALLAD OF READING GAOL AND OTHER POEMS, Oscar Wilde. 64pp. 27072-6

EARLY POEMS, William Carlos Williams. 64pp. (Available in U.S. only.) 29294-0

FAVORITE POEMS, William Wordsworth. 80pp. 27073-4

WORLD WAR ONE BRITISH POETS: Brooke, Owen, Sassoon, Rosenberg, and Others, Candace Ward (ed.). (Available in U.S. only.) 29568-0

EARLY POEMS, William Butler Yeats. 128pp. 27808-5

"EASTER, 1916" AND OTHER POEMS, William Butler Yeats. 80pp. (Available in U.S. only.) 29771-3

DOVER·THRIFT·EDITIONS

FICTION

FLATLAND: A ROMANCE OF MANY DIMENSIONS, Edwin A. Abbott. 96pp. 27263-X

SHORT STORIES, Louisa May Alcott. 64pp. 29063-8

WINESBURG, OHIO, Sherwood Anderson. 160pp. 28269-4

PERSUASION, Jane Austen. 224pp. 29555-9

PRIDE AND PREJUDICE, Jane Austen. 272pp. 28473-5

SENSE AND SENSIBILITY, Jane Austen. 272pp. 29049-2

LOOKING BACKWARD, Edward Bellamy. 160pp. 29038-7

BEOWULF, Beowulf (trans. by R. K. Gordon). 64pp. 27264-8

CIVIL WAR STORIES, Ambrose Bierce. 128pp. 28038-1

"THE MOONLIT ROAD" AND OTHER GHOST AND HORROR STORIES, Ambrose Bierce (John Grafton, ed.) 96pp. 40056-5

WUTHERING HEIGHTS, Emily Brontë. 256pp. 29256-8

THE THIRTY-NINE STEPS, John Buchan. 96pp. 28201-5

TARZAN OF THE APES, Edgar Rice Burroughs. 224pp. (Available in U.S. only.) 29570-2

ALICE'S ADVENTURES IN WONDERLAND, Lewis Carroll. 96pp. 27543-4

THROUGH THE LOOKING-GLASS, Lewis Carroll. 128pp. 40878-7

MY ÁNTONIA, Willa Cather. 176pp. 28240-6

O PIONEERS!, Willa Cather. 128pp. 27785-2

PAUL'S CASE AND OTHER STORIES, Willa Cather. 64pp. 29057-3

FIVE GREAT SHORT STORIES, Anton Chekhov. 96pp. 26463-7

TALES OF CONJURE AND THE COLOR LINE, Charles Waddell Chesnutt. 128pp. 40426-9

FAVORITE FATHER BROWN STORIES, G. K. Chesterton. 96pp. 27545-0

THE AWAKENING, Kate Chopin. 128pp. 27786-0

A PAIR OF SILK STOCKINGS AND OTHER STORIES, Kate Chopin. 64pp. 29264-9

HEART OF DARKNESS, Joseph Conrad. 80pp. 26464-5

LORD JIM, Joseph Conrad. 256pp. 40650-4

THE SECRET SHARER AND OTHER STORIES, Joseph Conrad. 128pp. 27546-9

THE "LITTLE REGIMENT" AND OTHER CIVIL WAR STORIES, Stephen Crane. 80pp. 29557-5

THE OPEN BOAT AND OTHER STORIES, Stephen Crane. 128pp. 27547-7

THE RED BADGE OF COURAGE, Stephen Crane. 112pp. 26465-3

MOLL FLANDERS, Daniel Defoe. 256pp. 29093-X

ROBINSON CRUSOE, Daniel Defoe. 288pp. 40427-7

A CHRISTMAS CAROL, Charles Dickens. 80pp. 26865-9

THE CRICKET ON THE HEARTH AND OTHER CHRISTMAS STORIES, Charles Dickens. 128pp. 28039-X

A TALE OF TWO CITIES, Charles Dickens. 304pp. 40651-2

THE DOUBLE, Fyodor Dostoyevsky. 128pp. 29572-9

THE GAMBLER, Fyodor Dostoyevsky. 112pp. 29081-6

NOTES FROM THE UNDERGROUND, Fyodor Dostoyevsky. 96pp. 27053-X

THE ADVENTURE OF THE DANCING MEN AND OTHER STORIES, Sir Arthur Conan Doyle. 80pp. 29558-3

THE HOUND OF THE BASKERVILLES, Arthur Conan Doyle. 128pp. 28214-7

THE LOST WORLD, Arthur Conan Doyle. 176pp. 40060-3